# The Greatest Performance

## Elías Miguel Muñoz

Arte Publico Press
Houston
Texas
1991

This volume is made possible through a grant from the National Endowment for the Arts, a federal agency.

Arte Publico Press
University of Houston
Houston, Texas 77204-2090

Cover design by Mark Piñón
Original painting by Benito Huerta:
"Premonition of Desire," Copyright © 1988

Muñoz, Elías Miguel.
    The greatest performance / Elías Miguel Muñoz.
        p.    cm.
    ISBN 1-55885-034-4
    I. Title.
PS3563.U494G74 1991
813'.54–dc20                                                91-9216
                                                            CIP

The paper used in this publication meets the minimum requirements of the American National Standard for Permanence of Paper for Printed Library Materials Z39.48-1984. ∞

To Tracy David Terrell, my Natural friend.

Thanks, Mari.

"I hope the exit is joyful"

Frida

# The Greatest
# Performance

# One

WE ARE IN CUBA, of course. In Guantánamo, to be more precise. My parents seem happy. Papi's a public accountant. Mami, a frustrated housewife. Doesn't she look beautiful in this picture? Mami doesn't seem to age. Papi, too, looks as handsome as he does today (in spite of his black-bean potbelly); velvety hair, dark complexion, features he says he inherited from his Castilian father.

They quarrel. He plays dominoes for money, she says. And he loses and loses. She's a watchdog, he claims. She spies on him, tries to control him. They hate each other's guts, but they stay together for the children. We need to have a normal set of parents, right? A nice home, a real family. And one day we will need to be freed from the communist tentacles.

You know how the story goes: This normal set of parents will have to leave their land to save their babies. And feeling fearful perhaps, or lonely, they will reinvent their matrimonial farce in the United States. Things will be better there, they think. They will have common goals and aspirations. He won't drink anymore. She won't be a bitch. And life will be a happily-ever-after.

But not yet. Not so easily. In a couple of years my brother Pedro is going to turn fourteen, military age. If they don't get him out before that, he'll never be able to leave. We can't take a chance waiting for our turn to enter the United States. So, fate has an unexpected voyage in store for my brother and me. Yes, I'll get to leave, too. But not to "America." We'll emigrate to Spain, thanks to a rich Spanish aunt who'll pay our way there.

Typical tale of a Cuban family of Worms, a decent home being torn apart. Rosita and Pedrito Rodríguez, two little twirps from Guantánamo who kneel by their beds every night and say their prayers, suddenly thrown into the world without their loving parents to protect them.

Our maternal grandmother, whom later in life I would baptize "La Filósofa," weeping and praying for our well-being, "May the Virgin of Charity protect you, children. May she guide your steps and keep you from danger. May she help you find your way back to us, some day." Our parents looking up at the blue Cuban sky and asking themselves, "Will we ever see our babies again?"

13

Later, in Garden Shore, our widow grandmother will amass a fortune from her Welfare and Social Security checks and will rent a two-bedroom apartment where she'll live by herself, free and independent, always a loving and faithful provider of *cafecito* and good old-fashioned Cuban wisdom. My parents will find assembly-line work in the aircraft industry, driven by the dream of buying a house with a garden, a swimming pool and a marble statue of the Virgin of Charity.

Yes, some dreams do come true.

★　★　★

Here's a picture of me at school: Rosita with her clique. The one with the curly red hair, that's Maritza. You can't see her face that well in this picture but believe me, she had the most bewitching bedroom eyes. And this is her wedding invitation. Pathetic, isn't it?

Maritza gave me little sermons about things that I couldn't and shouldn't understand: class struggle, the proletariat, Che, the capitalist pigs. She was a teacher's aide, strong in history and literature. And she spoke English. One day she'd go to the Soviet Union to study Russian, that was her plan. She wanted to read Tolstoy in the original.

She deserved her bookworm reputation, yes. But she was able to descend to my level and chitchat with me about trivialities; tube pants, miniskirts, popular music and groups like Los Bravos and Los Memes. And she translated for me the hit songs I liked that were in English, "Black is Black," "I'm a Believer," "Words."

I was a fairly good student. Good enough to have started high school a year earlier than I was supposed to. No, I wasn't a genius like Maritza; I had to study hard to get my Bs (eights and nines in the Cuban grade system).

I knew my geography from the North Pole to the South Pole. Well-acquainted with the Colonization period, I knew that when Christopher Columbus set foot in Cuba one day in 1492, he uttered the famous words THIS IS INDEED THE MOST BEAUTIFUL

LAND THAT HUMAN EYES HAVE EVER SEEN. I could recite by heart many of José Martí's *Versos sencillos* and name every single one of our Liberators, the men who fought for our (late) independence from the Spanish oppressors in 1898. (Too bad Martí had to be one of them).

I had read *Don Quijote*, *The Iliad* and *Romeo and Juliet*. I knew who Socrates, Aristotle, Shakespeare, Cervantes, Calderón, Marx, Lenin, Hemingway were. And I had definitely heard of the *Communist Manifesto*. I knew that Nikita was a good friend of Fidel's and that Johnson threw Black people to the dogs. And I chanted, like everybody else in town (before my family decided we would emigrate) that sing-song that went, "The Worms! (Feet thumping on the floor) Let's crush the Worms!"

★   ★   ★

Papi told me to be tough, "Don't let anyone intimidate you, Rosita. Your trip is not a crime." But no one treated me badly at school when I announced that I had received the "exit telegram." On the contrary, the principal had watery eyes when she hugged me. She told me to continue studying and not to let myself be trapped by the American vices. She was going to miss me, she said. And my classmates stared at me with puppy-dog eyes, as if I were traveling to a death camp and they were saying goodbye to me forever.

My only wish (I remember this clearly) was to stand in the middle of the school, right next to the flag, and to embrace Maritza, kissing her curly red hair and her lips. Telling her in front of the whole world that I loved her.

We walked to the park, I remember. And there we sat, in silence at first, then like two chatty parrots. And when it started to get dark, like two lovers saying *Adiós*, knowing they'd never see each other again.

My secret, impossible dream: that Maritza would come with me to the North, that she would abandon her communist family and escape to a land where dreams became reality. We would be free there. We'd go to school together and one day we'd buy a house at the beach and there we'd make our happy "nest."

I wrote to her a lot from California. I tried not to make a big deal of my brand new typewriter, my camera, my tape recorder, my color TV set, my family's car and the abundance of food. I told her of the music that was popular, Elvis, The Fifth Dimension, The Mamas and the Papas. I'd cut pictures of celebrities from the magazines and I'd send them to her.

There was little in my letters about Garden Shore, where we lived, about the Gringos and about my classes. All of that seemed unreal, uninteresting, a boring tale not worthy of telling. Her letters, the few that I got, were literary jewels. In the last one I received, and which I didn't answer, she sent me this wedding invitation ...

Pathetic, isn't it?

Seeing her name printed over a red heart, on that cheap cream-colored paper and next to the name of a man, MARITZA GARCIA & DAVID PEREZ, I felt for the first time that Cuba was vanishing from my life.

★   ★   ★

Look at this picture. See that cute guy there, in the back, behind Maritza? He's the one. My buddy. In my childhood story you have become that kid, Marito. Or rather, he has become you. And I can no longer remember his real name.

You live next door. We share a stereotypical biography: macho-father, puppet-mother. The Works. We help and comfort each other. You have a secret life similar to mine; we're accomplices. Best friends. But our friendship doesn't have a chance. My father has forbidden me to hang out with you because you're obvious, Marito. Blatantly obvious.

The first time you came to visit, my father didn't even greet you. Remember? And then when you left, his disgusting orders: "I never ever want to see you with that boy again! Can't you tell he's a *pájaro*?"

*Pájaro*. Bird. One of the words Cubans used in those days (still today?) to denigrate a gay man. What were some of the other ones? Ah yes, Duck, Butterfly, Inverted One, Sick One, Broken One, Little Mary, Addict, Pervert.

"I don't want to see you with that boy again, is that clear? Don't even speak to him!"

One day they started to pick up all the long-haired men, women
in miniskirts or hot pants, the whores, the ducks, and the dykes
(*Las Tortilleras*). Helterskelter, chopped off the ground as if they
were sugar cane. And you, my neighbor friend, were one of the
first to fall. Or did you escape The Raid? Were you as lucky as
me? No. I remember hearing the news at school, from Maritza:
"They got Mario. For being queer."

Even Julito Martínez, the macho dude who played the lead
in the country's most popular TV serial, *Zorro!*, had fallen. And
two of the singers who formed one of my favorite pop groups,
Los Memes, were gone, too. "What's going on?" I asked Maritza,
seeking comfort, some sort of affirmation in her wisdom. "Those
people are sick, Rosita," she responded. "And their sickness is
contagious."

How much pain we would've saved each other had we been
there together, at the genesis, for real. How much strength we
would've found in our friendship, Mario.

Truth is, I grew up alone in my lair, just like you.

No. It didn't happen overnight. I remember feeling attracted
to women since I was a baby. When I was seven I used to play
doctor with a neighbor girl. She'd hug me and I'd touch her "sick"
tummy and she'd touch the "bebé" I had between my legs and
it felt so good. We closed our eyes and kissed each other on the
mouth, kisses of tight and bumbling lips. We played house and I
was the husband. And we had children.

My fantasies started early. In them I was usually a handsome
knight in love with a princess. Or a tough militia man who carried
two guns, one hanging from each hip. A virile and feared lieutenant
(for some reason I never wanted to be a captain). Oh yes, and I
drove a jeep. Everyone respected me and loved me. Especially the
women. And I always managed to get the lady of my dreams.

I begged God to help me. Damn how I prayed! I'd kneel during
Mass and I'd tell Jesus Christ and the Virgin of Charity: Look,

here, please, you guys, pretty please, you've got to save my body
from temptation and my soul from eternal damnation. Tell you
what, so that everything goes fast and easy, I'll close my eyes and
I'll think real hard that I'm a normal girl and that I like boys. Then
I'll open my eyes, I'll look at the statue of Christ on the cross and—
Wham!—Rosita Rodríguez has been cured! She's a new person! Is
that a deal?

But there were no miracles for me.

Papi and Mami did nothing but argue and insult each other
and walk like zombies all over the house. He was drunk most
of the time. She'd do whatever she could do not to break down.
How could they possibly help me? And then there was my brother
Pedro, too much of a typical *machito* to understand how I was
feeling, or for me to trust him.

Mami did try to teach me the Cuban birds and bees. Was she
worried, perhaps, about my Tomboy look, my disdain for domestic
activities, my total apathy toward the opposite sex? She was determined, I could tell, to drive out of me all traces of masculinity,
to force me to be fragile, tender, womanly.

Lucky for me there were no beatings and no broken jaws, as
I know there were in other homes. From my sinful hideaway I
listened (I imagine now that I listened) to your cries. Things were
much worse for you, because you had been born a man. Your
crime deserved no forgiveness and no mercy.

Blows and kicks for you, The Butterfly. For me, advice: "Your
behavior must be ... calmer, Rosita. You should lower your voice
when you talk. You shouldn't be out there hunting birds and climbing trees. You should play house with your dolls and not play war
games with the boys. You must help me more around the house,
and stay home more. You should start wearing skirts. And you
should follow my advice ... "


Your mother threw a fork at you one day. She was having
lunch and you kept pestering her. What irked her about you that
morning? What were you bugging her about? I know, you wanted
her to tell you why she cried some times at night, "Does he hurt
you, Mima? Does he hurt you? Is that why you cry? Why do you
put up with him, Mima? Why do we put up with him?"

So she threw the fork at you. She didn't mean for it to hurt you; it was just an impulse, wasn't it? The fork punctured your arm, hanging there like a dead limb. The next day she started to direct traffic in the neighborhood. Would you say she went crazy? You got ten stitches and then you couldn't move your arm for a long time. Did seeing you hurting like that provoke her insanity? Was it remorse?

At the crack of dawn she'd put on your father's baseball cap and she'd hang a whistle from her neck. And there she went, stopping every car or pedestrian that passed in front of the house, blowing her whistle and giving bizarre orders, "Show me your identity. You can't go on unless you show me your identity." And people just cracked up in her face.

"What do I have to do to show you my identity?"

"Anything that would prove who you are."

The person (in most cases a man) would then make a gesture, sticking out his tongue or farting. "Very well," she'd respond, feeling accomplished, "you can go on, but carefully, don't forget that we are in the War Zone."

The fantasy ended abruptly one day, weeks later, when your father found out that a man had opened his fly to show your mother his enormous identity. Your Pipo nearly killed the guy. But why didn't he stop her from making a fool of herself from the very beginning? Why did he wait?

Did he want to laugh at her, too?

The school sent out a van to pick us up and take us home. You and I rode together the whole way, because we were in the same grade, and we were neighbors. I'm sure all the kids thought you and I were an item. Little did they know.

Why am I remembering this, Marito? Is it because ... there was something peculiar about you? Something I need to remember? Yes, you didn't like to go to the bathroom at school. How you managed to hold it all until you got home is beyond me, but you did. Until that afternoon, when we were sitting in the back and ... there was that nauseating smell. "What is this?!" asked the driver when he saw you getting out of the van. "This kid took a shit in his pants!" Everyone laughed and called you Shit Head and Dirty Asshole (or whatever the Cuban equivalents were, all of them having to do with the word *Mierda*).

You didn't go to the restroom at school because the prospect of exposing yourself in front of the other boys horrified you. (The toilet stalls didn't have doors.) But why? Was it because the ogre you had for a father punished you by making you take off all your clothes and then had you sit in the living room, stark naked? Was that the reason? Did you associate your nudity with punishment and pain?

I saw you there once, on the floor, in the middle of the living room, covering your parts and begging me with your eyes to end your torture, to leave perhaps, or bring you a blanket.

I'm sure I saw you naked once.

★   ★   ★

True, in most of my fantasies I was a man. But then there were those few occasions when I felt totally fem. When I would become *LA MUJER*.

My idol and role model for that fantasy was Rosita Fornés, the glamorous television queen, the greatest *artista*, the one and only Cuban star. Rosita was blonde and sexy and she sang heart-rending songs. She could dance and crack jokes and she had the body of a goddess.

It occurred to me during one of those fem fantasies that I should do Rosita Fornés' variety show in my backyard. Why not. I mean, wasn't it like destiny, like a mysterious fate that we both had the same name? (I asked Mami once if I had been named after the famous TV star, since Papi liked her so much and she was so famous and beautiful and maybe they wanted me to be famous like her some day. But Mima said absolutely not, that I had been named after Rosa María Fernanda Lucrecia Virginia, my great-grandmother on my father's side. *Coño!*) I could get some of my friends involved in the show, give them parts and songs to sing and funny things to say. And we could invite all the neighbors and charge money.

This artistic enterprise, I was sure, would be more profitable and far more successful than the lemonade sale, when there were so many lemons falling from the tree in our backyard that we didn't know what to do with them. "Make lemonade and sell it," Papi suggested. And I did. And I made enough money to buy three *Vanidades* and two *Bohemias*, all of them including lyrics of popular songs. But the ROSITA SHOW would top the lemonade sale; it would make neighborhood history. Or so I thought.

"Sing all you want," said Mami. "Sing Rosita's songs and do her dances. But no smooching. Understand?" What was she talking about? Rosita never kissed anybody in her TV show, or at least not that I'd noticed. And besides, did I have a tainted reputation? Quite the opposite, I was clean! But Mami's advice backfired. Yes, she put an idea in my head and in my heart, a wonderful idea for the show. We'd make it a love story, just like one of those Mexican movies that they showed on TV every day, where people talked about *El Amor* all the time, unrequited love, drunken love, betrayed love, sublime love. *El Amor*!

"And one more thing," Mami went on, "make sure you include Pedrito in your show. Just because he's little doesn't mean he doesn't have a right to have fun." My brother would eventually find his way into a thrillingly fun experience of his own. His wild awakening would come much later, in Spain. But that's another story.

We rehearsed outside, in the backyard, and Mami would spy on us through the kitchen window. We'd notice the tip of her nose, supervising, who knows if bored or fascinated, the rehearsal for our great melodrama, CARNIVAL QUEEN.

I'd play the female lead, of course. And you, Mario, would be my beloved and broken-hearted boyfriend Amor. You were a short and whitish boy, with light brown hair and unusually fine features. Perfect for the part of leading man. What I liked about you the most were your hands: impeccably white fingers, rosy nails; your dove-hands, Amor.

Dressed in pink with a fur coat I am La Rosa, a delicate ephemeral and desirable flower. I sing a song and then a fat old man gives me jewels and I accept them. Why not, all he wants from me is that I let him admire my beauty. Besides, the fatso's right: those jewels make me look radiant, more gorgeous than I am already.

We live in a village and it's Carnival time. I meet him one night, while I stroll through the plaza, watching the masquerading crowds. His name is Mario but I will call him Amor. We'll become sweethearts and he'll take me to his home, to meet his parents.

I walk in looking humble and average, wearing a simple summer dress, no jewelry and no fur coat. And his folks greet me; I am a decent girl and they are so pleased that their boy has met me. Because I go to Mass on a weekly basis. The sign of the cross and God bless you my child.

But then. Oh then. Amor finds out that I have a secret life, that I am the Carnival Queen. (How could I have possibly volunteered to play such a total fem?) He discovers me one night, half-naked, dancing my butt off on a majestic float.

Another dress, another song.

He cries because I'm not the decent girl he thought I was. I catch his glance full of sadness and rage. He runs, I jump off the float and run after him. I must tell him the truth! (I didn't know what that truth was, but I knew I had to explain it to him.) He runs to the pier and there he stops, and there I see him. He's thinking of jumping in; he's going to take his life! I scream, "No, Amor! Don't do it! Wait! You must listen to me, I am not who you think I am!" (But I really was, know what I mean?) Then there's a wave, a tidal wave that swells up and swallows him in one gulp. Amor! My love!

Another dress and the last song, *From the moment the day is born, to the moment when the sun dies, Amor, my love, I think of you. Amor, my love, you live in my heart ...*

"How about a happy ending" you asked. And you were right, Marito. We couldn't just leave the story hanging there with such a revolting, unoriginal *Fin*. So you came up with a great idea:

I'd go back to my glamorous float to dance my pain away and then one night, many years later, you'd show up. I'd see you smiling down below, in the crowd, still in love with me. You embrace me, and now we're both dancing on this magical float. And the float stops and the people gather around us. They listen to your story:

"A pirate ship picked me up and saved me from the sharks. I became a pirate and I sailed around the globe. I burned many houses and I stole many treasures. But then I repented from all those crimes and I came back searching for my Rosita. And now that we have found each other, I will no longer be a pirate. And she will no longer be The Carnival Queen, but only the Queen of my Heart. The End."

One evening, after our daily rehearsal, you brought me a plate of *mercocha*, that wonderful gooey stuff that Cuban mothers made from cooked sugar and cinnamon. "Here," you said, "my mother just made this ... for you." And right then and there you asked me timidly if you could give me a kiss, just a little kiss, you said. And I responded, "Of course, Marito, but not on the mouth, okay? Because that's for older people and, besides, I don't like to kiss boys." And you said, "Fantastic, Rosita, because I don't like to kiss girls but I'd love to kiss you, because you're my sister." And so you gave me this breathy kiss on the cheek and then I saw you blushing.

You shared your secret with me that evening. And I shared mine with you. You told me that you didn't like playing the handsome Amor, that who you really wanted to play was the Carnival Queen. I told you that if you ever played the Queen, some day, I'd play the leading man for you. Because deep down inside I didn't want to be her, that who I really wanted to be was Amor. And so you said, "Why do we have to wait? Why can't we do the show for ourselves, being the person that we want to be?" And we performed for each other, didn't we? And we fulfilled our wish.

The next day we announced to the "cast" that our show had been cancelled. The reason we gave our disillusioned friends was that the rehearsals were taking up too much of our time and we weren't doing our homework or studying enough. The real reason? You and I had already had our spectacular debut.

*   *   *

Here's a picture of me at the farm, which the Communists called "La Cooperativa." And that's my clique again. Don't I look like I'm having the time of my life?

Papi and Mami made such a fuss about my having to go work at La Cooperativa. Unfortunate little angel who had never had to lift a finger in her entire life, having to go break her back and soil her hands, working for the Bearded Serpent. Baby Rosita was going to be cleaning out furrows of sweet potato and cutting sugar cane for forty days! What an insult, what a slap in the face for my family.

But I loved the country. We had to work, yes, but not much; and we got slim and good-humored and playful. The saddest girls seemed to bloom at La Cooperativa.

We bathed together in a large hut that was ironically and properly named *Los Buenos Baños*, The Good Baths. My legs wobbled every time I went in there, I won't deny that. Tits tits tits. A room full of tits. But later, alone, I thought of someone special. Always about Maritza.

I know you didn't do anything "bad," you swear on it. But you were tempted. Oh how you were tempted! I imagine that the worst, the very worst torture you went through was the Cocks' Parade, *El Desfile de las Pingas*. How were you able to resist the temptation when you saw those giant *chorizos* willing, available, anxious and wasted? All those boys comparing each other, boasting about the shapes and sizes of their powerful erections; exploring each other to see who had the biggest, the thickest, the circumcised ones, the ones with more foreskin. Competing with each other by squirting their "milk" the longest distance. Or by breaking through a watermelon and parading around the barracks with the fruit hanging from their sex. Let's see who can hold it up the longest!

The most difficult test was the one you endured with Paquito, wasn't it? Paquito, the barber's son, had a habit of offering you tidbits of wisdom for survival: "Never be a tattletale. Never. Be anything you want except a tattletale. Be a cocksucker, a ball-licker, a Duck, a Little Mary. Bend down and spread your cheeks, but don't be a tattletale. No one here's gonna treat you bad for being a queer. But if you're a tattletale you'll get killed, we'll cut you up with a machete." Minutes later he opened his fly and displayed a long and dark and wrinkled pecker. "Suck it, I won't tell anyone. I'm not a tattletale."

You said no, trembling inside, resisting the temptation like a true hero. "Suck it, I know you want to," the barber's son insisted. But you didn't.

You didn't dare.

Maritza and I had a reunion at La Cooperativa. It was kind of magical, if you can believe that. She had been distant and aloof at school. Afraid of me, maybe. Afraid of being picked up or contracting my contagious "illness"?

She smiled at me again when we got to the country. And we ended up talking a lot about music. Our latest idol was Armando Manzanero, the Mexican singer-songwriter. He had a hideously romantic voice, an unbearably touching falsetto. And his words, oh his words! He sang of rainstorms and lonely crowds and forsaken lovers and adoring lovers and forever-ever-lovers.

I knew every one of Manzanero's songs. I could imitate his high-pitched voice, the exact modulation of his notes, the violin part, the piano solos. Inevitably, I ended up serenading Maritza whenever I had the opportunity. One morning, much to my surprise, she asked me if I would sing for her in private, "Where no one can hear you. Sing only to me." My mouth dropped.

I suggested we go to the plantain field after dawn. And we did. And as soon as we were out of sight I kissed her. Then we walked holding hands, laughing, discussing her favorite books (*War and Peace, Don Quijote*), my favorite movies (*Fantomas, Jotavich*); talking about us; about being friends forever. And about my singing. She said I had a pretty voice, that I should try to sing professionally. But I couldn't, I said, I wouldn't want to sing anymore if she were not around to hear me.

We were far from the barracks when I asked her to sit down, to lean against the trunk of a tree and relax, close her eyes and just let herself dream. Softly I said, "We're alone. And I'm going to serenade you." And then I saw that from behind the tree appeared this woman, this woman who sang, entranced, *We are sweethearts,* who whispered, *because we feel this love, sublime and profound.* She hummed, she sang, *This love that makes us proud.* She cried, *This love so weary of goodbyes.* She pleaded, *Come hear, come hear my sweetheart's lullaby.*

# Two

I'M HOLDING HIS HAND. There are crowds and tall buildings, white columns, glass doors. I cling to him, straggling behind, frightened. Why does he push me away? I look up at his moustache, I don't see it. And the woman by his side doesn't have short hair like Mima, but she's pretty and she smiles and she wants to know my name. "Marito," I tell her. She says I must be lost.

People go by. They don't notice my tears. Where's my Pipo? Will I ever hide in his arms again? Will I fall asleep on his pillow, tie his shoe laces, hear his laughter because I make too many knots, open his briefcase where he keeps *chicles* for me, see him smoke his cigars? I long to hear his voice, the love songs he sings in the shower, throw sand on his chest and go fetching sea shells with him, let him carry me on his shoulders so that I can dive into the water from up there. Where? Where is my Pipo?

I see him. I run to him. I hug him hard, as if afraid that he might leave again. He tells me that it was all a prank, that I shouldn't cry, "Tears are for sissies." He had been hiding from me to see my reaction.

◇　◇　◇

Mima helped me write the letter. I asked for a bicycle, a train, crayons and coloring books, a watercolor set, a life-size doll that you could wind up and then it would walk and eat; better a male doll, because that way I could pretend he was my brother. And I could give him my name, Marito.

I imagined the Three Wise Men riding their camels and wearing pointed boots, the type people wore in the movie *Aladdin and the Magic Lamp*; cloaks and layered garments of lights. It made me happy to think about them, Melchior, Gaspar and Balthasar, to imagine them walking into my house after having flown through the clouds, traveling leagues and leagues from a distant country hidden in Heaven.

I was already wide awake when Pipo and Mima came to get me.

They hugged me and we went to the living room and then I couldn't make up my mind where to run first. There were toys hanging from the walls. The furniture was covered with them, too. And in the middle of the room, on the floor, there was a train running wildly, surrounded by mountains and lakes and green grass. And there were robots and brand new shoes and coloring books of all types and sizes and boxes of crayons, and pencils, watercolors, tubes of oil paint that looked just like little stuffed frogs. And there were baseballs and bats and gloves and trucks and cars and war tanks. There were lions, tigers, monkeys, zebras, giraffes, horses, dogs, cows, bulls, sheep, kangaroos, and doves with their nests and eggs and everything ...

"And my toy-brother?"

I hugged my pillow. I took the mosquito net off. I asked Mima for two more pillows. But I couldn't, I just couldn't fall asleep. My pacifier was lost and we hadn't been able to find it. She said she'd buy me a new one, same shape and color. But I wanted my old one, and I started to accuse her of having hidden it from me. Then I accused Pipo, because he always said that I was too big to still be sucking that thing and that one of these days he was going to burn it.

The next morning Mima told me a story. She said that she had seen the hand of an angel moving through my mosquito net during the night, and the hand had taken my pacifier away. Then a beautiful white face with blonde ringlets had told her that I should now grow up and become a man.

I had a vision, too, of that same blonde angel, that night. And I smacked it so hard that it swirled around the room several times. I cussed it out, ordering it to give me back my pacifier. But the angel didn't obey me. And the second time I smacked it it swooned, vanishing forever.

Zenaida cried a lot the day of the quarrel, when the stick fell on her head. It was one of those long, varnished pieces of wood that we used to prop up the mosquito net.

Zenaida was kind to me. She would rock me in a huge chair that had a wicker back with tiny holes in it. She'd close her eyes and start rocking me by my bedroom door, and then she'd open her eyes and there we were, in the living room! "How did this happen, Marito?!" She'd pretend to be surprised, having moved the chair herself, gradually, over the slippery wood floor. "How did we end up over here?!" I couldn't stop laughing.

In the midst of the quarrel—Mima weeping in the kitchen, Pipo pushing and shoving and throwing every object that came into his field of vision—I made an attempt to attack him, grabbing the shiny stick and hitting him with it. Up there, close to the ceiling, rose his double chin, his thin moustache, his *guayabera*, his enormous hairy arms.

I saw Zenaida crying. And then I saw Pipo dropping the stick on her head. I went for his legs, biting them. He dragged me by the arms all the way to my room, "Sit down and don't move!"

That afternoon he took me to the park and told me that he was going to buy me any toy I wanted. Which he did. Lots of toys.

But after the day of that quarrel, Zenaida never came back.


Mima would wake me up and then I'd run to the kitchen, where I would stand watching the bags full of goodies for our weekend trip to Guantánamo Beach.

Pipo would rent a cabin on the sand, by the water. I loved the beach but I hated the fact that those cabins didn't have a restroom; you had to go to the public baths to clean yourself. That was embarrassing. Pipo insisted on both of us using the same shower stall, so he could scrub me hard, the way little boys needed to be scrubbed. Men with long things and boys with tiny ones would pass by and stare, pointing at the father-and-son shower spectacle.

After going through that ordeal we were usually greeted by Mima, who waited for us with a feast, under a pine tree, on one of those tables made of freshly-cut wood, where you could count every single ring. Mima explained to me that each one of those rings was a year in the life of the tree. Once we counted ten rings. The tree had died, I was sad to find out, when it was the same age as me.

The floor had red tiles and the table was long. The chairs were upholstered in goatskins. The hair seemed so real that whenever you sat down, you had the impression you were sitting on a live beast.

Pipo did business with some shop that made belts and he'd had that back room built to store his merchandise. I'd take my coloring books and my crayons and spend hours there, sitting on the boxes that were piled up on the floor. But I never closed the door. Pipo had forbidden me to do that.

He told me the story of a boy who liked to scare his poor parents by shutting himself up inside a little room like this one. "Save me!," the boy would call for help, "I'm being eaten by a spider!" And his parents ran to help him. Then the kid would stick his tongue out at them and laugh in their faces. Until one time when the kid started to scream, sounding more anguished and desperate than ever before, and his parents didn't run to his rescue. The boy stopped crying eventually. And his parents found him, much later, in the stomach of a boa constrictor. The animal seemed inflated and stuffed. You could discern the shape of the boy's body in its belly.

⋄   ⋄   ⋄

It's raining hard. Loud thunder. My window has been bolted; the bolt we use for storms. I pull aside the curtain and I can see the patio through the window. The evil wind is bending the trunk of the tamarind tree. Its leaves are gone, its fruits flying in Heaven.

Knocking. The sounds of the storm? There it is again, so close, in here, in my own room. "Who is it? Who wants in? Get away! Whoever you are, get away!" His face outside, I see it. His dripping face, freezing. I struggle with the heavy bolt. I can't, I can't get it to open! But I must keep on trying. His imploring eyes are telling me, "Help me. I am cold. Let me in."

And I do, I let him in. The bolt finally gives. He stumbles as he jumps into my bedroom. "What's your name?" I ask him. "You don't need to know my name," he murmurs, cuddling up next to me. He seems to be my age, but he doesn't have my ash-brown hair and light complexion. He's dark, skinny, taller than me. He has black curly hair and dimples when he smiles. And he's smiling now. "I was very cold," he says. I hug him, "You won't be cold anymore."

Music from the radio in the living room. Or is it Pipo singing in the shower? Beautiful melody. A distant echo that transports me, that takes me up among the clouds, that drops me into this bed of sponge where my new friend sleeps, safe from the storm.

I can't do it. What if they find us. He'll kill me. He won't? You promise? I shouldn't be afraid. You will protect me. Give me your hand, don't let me slip and fall. Wait for me! I'm getting soaked to the skin. Here I go! I'm jumping out!

The raindrops are thick and sweet, like coconut water; they splash against my forehead. Under the tamarind tree. Dark clouds, a body of leaves. Dense mist through which I see his thin, fine fingers like the legs of a spider, the white palms of his hands. Puddles and mud. Tadpoles. Garments that smell of cilantro. I'm free.

◇   ◇   ◇

Three policemen broke into Pipo's back room and made a mess. And they took Pipo away, handcuffed. When he came back, he was skinny and smelled bad, his clothes were wrinkled. That day he started to make plans for us to move. He bought an empty lot on the outskirts of town, and sent for magazines from Miami so we could select the perfect American model for our house.

We were having dinner in our brand new chalet, months later, when he told us that things were getting bad in the country, that he couldn't do his work anymore. The new government had appropriated the shop and now he couldn't sell his belts. And not only that. Now we'd have to explain and justify every one of our moves and thoughts to some black scum family that had moved to our neighborhood, claiming to be the Committee for the Defense of the Revolution.

We had to get the hell out of Cuba, he said. His friends in Miami would help us. We'd be better off in the North.

Kids from the neighborhood came to watch TV in our house. Pipo had warned me the day he brought home the set; and so had Mima, that I shouldn't invite anyone, that I shouldn't tell any of the neighbors that we had a brand new TV. But I told everybody.

The kids marveled at the porcelain vases and glass figurines and all the expensive furniture that crowded our home. I guess they couldn't understand how a wealthy family like us had ended up building a mansion in this part of town, where mostly poor people lived. Come to think of it, I didn't understand either.

One of the women who came to watch TV with her children said, once, that she'd be happy with only half of the things we owned. Just then it dawned on me: we were rich.

The serial starts at seven. *Zorro*! *Avenging and righteous Zorro*! And it is fifteen to seven. I have shut the living room door and windows. I hear their knocks and cries; the show is about to start, "Open up, Marito! Let us in!"

*She has begun to suspect that Diego is the righteous and valiant Zorro, even if he continues to act like a sissy.*

*Because she just found him at the mouth of the cave that runs under the mansion, the one that leads to the library. He speaks to her in a deep, virile voice, and cracks his whip; his horse neighs.*

No show.

*She tells him, "Thank you, Diego," calling him by his real name, "thank you for helping us."*

*"Now that you know the truth," he says, "nothing will stop me."*

*"Watch out for yourself, Diego!"*

*"I will come back for you."*

*"Don't leave."*

*"I have to. But not for long."*

*"I love you, Diego!"*

*"Tonight this town will witness the last appearance of Zorro!"*

There will be no show tonight, not with this swollen face.

No show.

The bean soup burns my tongue, I blow on it. Pipo tells me to stop and to eat it. "It's not that hot," he says. I soak the bread in the broth. Trying to get comfortable, I straddle the chair as if it were a horse. He's staring at me. He pulls the tablecloth and my soup spills. He throws a piece of bread at me. He pinches the inside of my thighs, hits my chest. He grabs me by the hair and pokes my stomach with his fingers. "Men don't sit that way, shit!" he yells. "Only broads sit that way, so they can air out their pussies!"

In my room, he tears up my drawings and pushes my face into the watercolor set, forcing me to eat my greens, my reds and blues and grays, my pinks and my browns, the spots of colored water, the fine hair of my brushes.

"Eat it all. Eat it!"

◇   ◇   ◇

But you were the one, Pipo, the one who took me to Hernando's farm. You asked me to go with you. Because Hernando had a plantain field and he was selling his stuff on the black market. And you could buy a lot of plantains and I could help you carry them home.

After our trip to Hernando's farm, Hernando would ride his bike in front of our house every day; sometimes he stopped in. And he would stay for a while watching TV with me and Mima. She would always make coffee for him. He seemed like a kind man.

He showed up one afternoon looking disturbed. The government was going to appropriate his farm, he said, and he wouldn't be able to sell his merchandise to us anymore. If we wanted to buy a last couple of bunches, this was the time to do it. Now. But one of us would have to go with him to fetch the stuff.

Mima said that her husband wasn't home, and that it wasn't right for her to go to the farm. Unfortunately, we'd have to pass up the opportunity. So Hernando suggested that I be the one to make

e purchase. I was strong enough to help him cut the bunches and
bring them back, he told Mima. He'd give me a ride on his bike.
And Mima thought that was an excellent idea. I should get ready,
she ordered me, put on my tennis shoes and accompany Hernando.
My Pipo, she added, my Pipo would be very proud of me.

When I go out to the porch, Hernando's already waiting for me
on his bike. His pants are large and baggy; he rolls them up. He
says I must hold on tight to his stomach, otherwise I'd fall. Hold
on tight to his waist. Soft, rubbery stomach just like yours, Pipo.
*Hold on tight.*

His nervous tic and his relentless coughing. Straight black hair,
thin eyebrows. Aquiline nose and lipless mouth. Not as tall as
you, Pipo. But hairy arms just like yours.

Another boy comes to see him, he says. And they do things.
From a long time ago, he tells me, they've been doing little things.
I remind him of that boy. He knew I was a *pájaro*, a queer, from
the very moment he laid eyes on me, the day I came to his farm
with my father and I acted like a sissy, refusing to get my feet
dirty with mud and complaining about the weight of the plantain
bunches. Those plantains were heavy for a kid like me, they sure
were.

He says he knows I am in need of a man. Kids like me need
special protection, we're delicate and fragile like girls, weaker even,
and only someone like him, Hernando, can provide that special
attention we require. I will always be a baby, he tells me, that's
my role in life. Even when I grow up, I will always see myself that
way, as an obedient child.

And he's willing to be my protector.

Have I ever had sex with a real man, he wants to know. Not
other kids like me or older boys, that's just playing. He means
a real man with big balls and a huge dick, *un pingón*, a man who
fucks women. No, I have never done anything with anybody. Well,
he's happy to hear that, because he knows just how to do it. And
he wants to teach me. He's a man of his word; he promises me
he'll never tell on me. He'll never say, Yeah, look at him, he's a
faggot and he gives me his ass. Never. I can trust him.

Most of all, I shouldn't be afraid.

I hobble over the puddle in front of the door and dirty my shoes. A small and cluttered room. No windows. Clothes everywhere and an unmade cot. Next to the cot a large scale where he places me, grabbing me by surprise and lifting me. He wants to know how much I weigh. Not much, but I have tender full flesh; I eat well, he can tell. He touches my legs, my back, my arms.

"And if you let me," he says, "stick my hand under your shirt, just a little bit, like this, you see. If you let me, I swear I'll do anything for you, Marito. What a good boy you are, letting me touch you under your shirt. Now you must let me touch you down here, unbuckle your belt, nice belt, yes, back here, your little round cheeks, so soft and warm. And now if you touch me just a little, give me your hand, put it here, see? If you touch me just a little, I swear I'll do anything for you, boy. Leave your hand there for a while, yes, like that. Now you can move it inside. The fly is open, try it. Put your hand inside, that's good. It's hard, isn't it? Let's bring it out, I'm going to take a pee. You want to see me doing it? I can pee far, into the puddle, watch me. Look at this, how red the head is getting under the sun. I'll pull the skin all the way back, look how it moves, and then the head gets bigger; it swells up. You lick it with your tongue, like you're tasting *mercocha*, like this, watch my mouth when I lick my arm. Got it? You do it like that. Yeah, that's my boy. What a nice little tongue you have. Smooth and pink. I swear I'll do anything for you, Marito. Anything ... "

I want to wash my hands and he points to the makeshift wash-basin outside, full of soiled water. I want soap; he doesn't have any.

I ask him why he doesn't have a bathroom in his room; he says that he'll have one made for me. Because I'm going to come back to see him, right? He will give me a bike for my trips and I will come back as many times as he wants me to. We made a pact, he reminds me. I need him and he's going to help me.

I tell him I never want to see him again, and he warns me not

to contradict him; he could get mad and smack me, he tells me.
Do I like getting smacked? He should've split my ass in half, he
shouts, instead of being kind and gentle. He should've made me
bleed. But no, he likes me, he doesn't want to hurt me. All I have
to do is return once in a while so I can suck his thing.

"One day we're going to have a real fuck and you're going to
love it, kid. Like having all of your insides caressed, that's how it
feels. As simple and delicious as that," he says.

◇    ◇    ◇

The stench of beer served in paper cups. Reflectors and stream-
ers, fake palm trees, papier-mâché flowers. Behind the floats, the
Guantánamo people. One massive masked body moving to the
rhythm. *Guapachá* And I swing and sway, letting myself be carried by the movement, *Guapachá*! sweating, singing, dancing.

"I know who you are!" I hear his voice. "I know who you are
behind that mask!" His carnival face, drenched in sweat. "Who
am I?" He takes my hand and drags me to a clear spot on the
sidewalk, in front of a shop window. The white palms of his hands
rest on the glass; he observes the reflection of my masked face.
"Who am I? Tell me."

I can't recognize him because he's older now, he says, just like
I'm older, too. But beautiful memories don't die when you grow
old. He tells me of a storm and a tamarind tree. He still loves me.

He's become a dancer. Did I see him moving like a demon on
top of the float with a mountain? The tallest of all floats, with a
perfect replica of Turquino Peak. He helped build it and it took all
year. Did I see him? His rumba steps. A personal show for me, I
deserve it. I shared my bed with him when he was down and out
and soaking wet. He will never forget me.

The asphalt street ends and now we skip over dents and puddles. We turn right to find a narrow street, then a narrower one,
an alleyway. We march along the huts, smelling the fried pork and
the garbanzo soup.

We turn right again when we get to a kiosk. There, that's where
he lives, behind the kiosk. "Not bad for a poor dancer," he says.

He unbolts the lock and invites me in. We enter a small room vaguely illuminated by a kerosene lamp, crowded with a table that's too large for it and some chairs.

His face in chiaroscuro as he stands next to the window: "Yes, I remember you now." A beautiful melody. A distant echo taking me up to the clouds. His playful silhouette emerging from the darkness and the silence. I can sense him again, next to me, safe from the storm and the cold. His furtive steps, his body writhing through my sheets as if they were a warm coconut-water stream.

There's a kind man who helps him out now and then, "He gave me a brand new bike ... And he feeds me." Do I want to meet him? No, I already have a bike and plenty to eat. "What's his name?" I ask him. "Hernando," he answers.

◇   ◇   ◇

The alarm clock in her bedroom; damned buzzer. Her feet will slide into the rubber sandals. Her bulging body will slip into a flowered robe. Her hand on my forehead, "Wake up, Marito." She'll be waiting for me in the kitchen, at the table, with breakfast ready.

I get into the bathtub and a frog jumps out, the usual morning frog hiding in the shower curtain. I will sing a mushy *bolero*, like Pipo, while I scrub hard ... *Lover, if only I had a heart* ... Later, I'll dip the buttered bread in the coffee with milk, and Mima will tell me about the things she'll do today. Some sewing, maybe. Or maybe nothing at all.

In line. Your hand to your temple, the right side. And the blue-and-white-striped flag, *La Bandera*, hoisted on top of the world, *To the frontline, Guantánamo men. Your motherland is proud of you, Guantánamo men* ...

My desk, the third one in the row closest to the wall. Who will they pick on today? On one of the fat guys, always the fat guys. Carlos the hick, *El Guajiro*, nine-months belly: "Who's the macho father who managed to break through the pig's lard?" Or Heriberto, *El Gordo*, who ended up throwing up on the teacher's feet one day, after taking weeks of abuse: "Evacuate! Evacuate!"

And then the class clowns trying to decipher the fatso's vomit: "Rice with chicken," they notice tiny white grains. "Avocado too," they stare at the greenish black chunks." "A bull frog!" they point to a blob with beady eyes, amphibian legs and bulging tummy. Heriberto El Gordo being carried by ten guys to the infirmary: "Moby Dick on board!" Then the poor teacher, Señorita Ramírez, having to clean up the mess.

Pieces of chalk shattering against the blackboard; a pencil breaks in half over somebody's head. Señorita Ramírez approaching! "Did you read the *Versos sencillos*, class? Her watery, blood-shot eyes; her greasy black hair parted in the middle, "Very well, then. You, Mario, recite one for us, if you'll be so kind."

*I am an honest man from where the palm tree grows. And before I die, I want to share these verses of my soul ... Guantanamera! Guajira Guantanamera ...*

Her everpresent dress, her orthopedic shoes, perfectly tied laces; the thick vein that popped up on her neck, on the verge of explosion, when she talked about our school. A lump in her throat, half-uttered words when she talked about our school born to this holy Revolution. Free and sovereign, our school, like its students and its teachers, like the citizens of this exemplary land. Our revolutionary school.

She's waving a sheet of paper in the air: "El Che is gone, my young comrades, but he has left us this letter." She will read it to us, "This is his legacy." She'll make an effort to refrain from crying, "*The faith that you inculcated in me, Fidel ...* His work is done in Cuba. El Che must now go and wage other much-needed battles and free other people from their yoke ... He planted his seed in our soil, my young comrades. He'll always be the valiant spirit of our Revolution ...

"*Until victory, always ...* "

I could stay at school for lunch, go to the kiosk around the corner and have a mamey shake. Or buy cookies from the fat lady who doesn't wear bloomers and has a deep belly button like a crater that shows through the fabric of her dress; the woman who stations herself with her metal cookie box by the principal's door, sprawled over a makeshift stool like a big white octopus. "Ten for a nickel! Ten for a nickel!" Her cookies are sweet and they dissolve in your mouth.

I could stay at school, instead of taking the bus and going home for lunch, and talk to Antonio. Lately the guys have been teasing me a lot about Antonio. They say he's got the hots for me, that he's after my buns, my *nalguitas*. But I don't think so.

I like Antonio's hair, dense and tangled, his brown face, his green eyes, his Adam's apple. I like his hairless arms and the way he walks, self-assured. Antonio is smart, the only one of us who really knows English. The only one who speaks, confident, fluent, with the teacher. I call him Mister Anthony. But he doesn't like that name. He tells me to shut up whenever I say it.

We're walking home; he doesn't live far from school. Lucky me, walking with Mister Anthony. "Why don't you let your hair grow long?" I ask him. "Let the bangs cover your forehead, the way the Beatles wear it, the way I wear it?" Because, he says, men are not supposed to have bangs. Bangs are for queers and for crazy rock singers, not for him.

I have been collecting song lyrics, all the Manzanero songs, I have them. Does he want to see them? Wouldn't he like to sing those songs with me some time? They're so romantic ... No, he wouldn't. I'll make him a drawing of whatever he wants; his most favorite thing in the world, I'll draw it for him. But no, he wants nothing from me. "Leave me alone," he demands.

Why? I don't have a plan, a secret scheme. I don't want his protection or his brown dick or his hairy balls. I don't want him to do to me what Hernando has been doing to me for months. I swear I don't. Maybe touching his hair, running my fingers through it; maybe touching his neck, his Adam's apple, maybe holding his hand. His friendship.

He hits my face and kicks me. He pushes me against a wall. Will he talk? Will he say anything? Or will he just go on kicking my legs, driving his feet into my stomach?

"I told you to leave me alone!," he says finally. "I told you to get out of my way. Go find yourself another macho to fuck you. You faggot!"


◇   ◇   ◇


Chalet painted in light flamingo. The porch: slanted columns of sharp edges; a patio and a back yard; a rose garden; an orchard;

a carless garage. The most modern house in the neighborhood, right out of the American pictures.

The radio serial: A prince and a princess and an evil witch. Impossible love. After the hour-long fairy tale there will come a show called *Sorpresa Musical*. From the patio, a penetrating smell of boiled clothes; the laundry woman and her daughters, cackling. In the kitchen the pressure cooker squeaks. Garbanzo stew, I loath the smell. On my desk drawings of male models copied from *Bohemia* and *Vanidades*. And a masculine voice from the radio, deep and resonant, promising a musical surprise. *We are sweethearts*, he whispers, *because we feel this love, sublime and profound*. He sings, he whispers, *This love that makes us proud*. He cries, *This love so weary of goodbyes*. He pleads, *Come hear*, he hums, *Come hear my sweetheart's lullaby*.

Young militia man, *El Miliciano*: "These papers say that you folks want to leave the country. Is that correct?"

"Yes, that's correct."

"In that case, I'll have to inventory your belongings."

"Yes. We know."

"I'll have to make a list of everything you own, even the water-color set and the boy's drawings."

"We know."

The Miliciano will order the man of the house to go to the fields, to cut sugar cane. The man of the house will live there, in Las Barracas, until the time comes for him and his family to leave. The time when the family receives the exit telegram. Sunday at six in the morning, Guantánamo Park: "You must cut a lot of sugar cane, comrade."

Pipo's willing to pay the price. The sacrifice is worth it if he can get the fuck out of here. He'll work for these bastards, break his back for these bastards. He'll live in filth if he has to, surrounded by hicks and niggers. He'll put up with it all so that one day Fidel grants us exit and sends us the telegram. He'll do whatever he has to.

Now we're the Worms, *Gusanos*. That's what they call us. And we're willing to kiss the Gringo asses. Sell ourselves. Turn ourselves into whores.


I'll have to do my share of labor when my school goes to the country for forty days. The Revolutionary Law: Students and teachers must contribute to the process, offer their hands and their time; they must experience the *campesino* life. *Campesinos*, the peasants, sustain us; they are the blood of our history. We must help them. We owe them this much.

But what about Pipo? They took him to Las Barracas, where all the traitors are being taken to receive their punishment. Faggots are taken there, too, because the Revolution says they're sick and need reforming, treatment. Pipo may have to sleep next to a *pájaro*. Pipo may be doing it to him. Could he? No. Pipo has no prick, nothing to do it with. The Pipo I love has no sex; like the blonde angel who stole my pacifier, he has nothing to put inside a boy's ass. So he's safe.

Am I safe? Hernando says they'll never catch me, that I don't look that effeminate. And besides, I'm too young. But I know my youth is no guarantee; the young ones are being picked up, too. The ones with long hair and bangs, the ones who wear makeup, the ones who sing Beatle songs, the ones with tight pants. Even the women, the ones people call *Tortilleras*, they are being taken to Las Barracas. A magical site where sick men and women turn normal and the deserters pay their dues, Las Barracas.

My Pipo has no chance for survival there, he's too weak. The Pipo I know has never hit anybody, much less his own son, and he has never flaunted his huge dick; he has a tiny one. The Pipo I know sings love songs in the shower. He doesn't boast about his strength, doesn't test it out on a little boy's face. He's weak. Right?

His blood will rot in Las Barracas; his skin will dry up and crumble like a cornhusk. He will turn invisible, or green like the underbrush, red like the earth underneath his feet. Bitten by infected mosquitoes. Or butchered by an angry communist machete; pushed down a cliff by envious hands; strangled by a venomous snake; shot in the heart by a demented lover of innocent boys. Alone. And lonely.

Right?

◊   ◊   ◊

Sunset of bleeding reds and shadows on the crystal-blue surface. The ceiling pulls me, propels me and pulls me. My neck cracks against the ceiling beams. Under my feet, a bridge of rotting logs, sharks down below. A sewer of dead children. Where I fall ...

Your arms used to embrace me. There, in front of a window that covered half the wall, next to me, in my bed, you used to kiss me. In my white and always burning bed, your head on my clean pillow, your smell on my smell. Who am I? Who am I now but you, Pipo. And you are me.

I just heard you come in. You're tiptoeing your way to my tiny plump arms. Please come, rest by my side, lie down. Cuddle up to me. Let me caress your peaceful eyelids, watch you sleep. Oh let me love you again, Pipo.

# Three

"WE'VE GOT TO GET HIM OUT!" said Papi. "Before the military pigs get him!" He was referring to Pedro. My brother ran a risk, I didn't. I was the *niña*, and at the time females were not required to do time in the Cuban service. Ideally, though, we would both get out.

The plan: A rich spinster aunt from Madrid, Tía Lola, would lend us the money for the trip to Spain. And she would "claim" us. We'd stay with her for a few days. Then we'd have to go to Casa de Campo, the children's shelter where most Cuban kids traveling alone ended up going. Our aunt was too old and couldn't take care of us. We'd be on our own, basically.

★　★　★

An old woman opened the door and asked us to come in, showing us to a room which Pedro and I thought was a museum. "Wait here, please," she said in Castilian. And as she was leaving the room, "Sit down!" she ordered. We sat and peered around, staring at the many paintings; at one especially, of a young woman in Flamenco dress and wearing a *peineta*. Our aunt when she was young?

When Tía Lola finally showed up, we had the impression we were facing a ghost. She was pale, frail, and had tiny feet that were stuck in high-heeled shoes and shaped like meat hooks. She walked in limping and pinched Pedrito's cheeks, caressed my head and sat between us. She gave us each a distant, whispered kiss. She smelled of old clothes and perfume.

"You're both so handsome!" she pinched my cheek this time. "Did you have a good trip?" We nodded yes. "Did you like traveling in an airplane?" We nodded again. "It was incredible we couldn't believe it," babbled Pedrito. "It was like we had never thought it would be, you know, because we were up there in the air and some day I want to be a pilot and fly really high and go up to the clouds and ... " I clamped my hand over his mouth, "You're talking too much, Pedrito!" But Tía Lola seemed pleased by my

47

brother's aeronautical fantasy. "Yes, yes," she said. "It must be fantastic. I have never traveled by plane myself. And now I know I never will. I'm too old." She touched Pedro's tummy. "Are you hungry?" He opened his eyes wide and uttered a loud and honest *Sí!*

"Wait one moment, then." She got up and left. Seconds later we heard her shrill voice coming from a room that I took to be the kitchen, "You can't do anything right! How could you be so stupid, woman!" She was talking to her maid, I assumed.

Never had I felt as alone and forsaken as I did at that moment. Our ride to the Havana airport; Mami wearing ridiculous dark-tinted sunglasses, hiding her tears, silent. Papi who had suddenly become a little boy, wanting to cry and not knowing how to do it. Abuela, sobbing and weaving philosophical tales to comfort us, "There is a plan, children. Everything happens for a reason. All of this was meant to be ... "

Our Iberia flight. The air, inside the jet, which was no longer the warm Cuban air. The coldness I felt when I stepped out of the jet. Freezing October cold. The smell of burned lard inside the airport. The sunless sky.

Sitting there, waiting for Tía Lola, I didn't know whether I'd ever see Mami, Papi or Abuela again. Pedrito by my side, confused and terrified. "She looks like a mummy!" he cried out.

"Sshh! She'll hear you, Pedro." He got up and headed for the door. "I don't want to live here, with that mummy." I dragged him back to the couch, "Sit down and shut up!" He sat reluctantly. "She looks like a dead frog!"

Tía Lola came back followed by her servant, who was carrying a tray of Spanish delicacies: tiny sandwiches, pastries of all shapes and colors, cheese, fruits, candy. "This woman!" wailed Tía Lola, "this woman takes forever to do everything!" She sat with us again and waited for the maid to serve us all. "The biggest plate is for Pedrito!," she announced, smiling. "He's the hungriest boy in the world!" She nibbled at some of the things she was served while my brother and I fed our faces eagerly and aggressively. "You kids eat all you want," she said as she got up. "There's much more inside." And she left again.

I walked to the balcony and opened the glass door. I went outside, feeling stuffed, breathing in the cold air. "What in the world are you doing out there?!" I heard my aunt yelling. "You'll catch a cold and then you'll surely give it to me and I can't afford to be sick, at my age, I can't run such risks! Come in, for Heaven's sake! And put on your coat!"

I came back in. "Didn't you bring a coat?" she asked, and we showed her the coats our grandmother had made from old thick blankets. "We'll have to buy you new clothes," she stated, glancing disdainfully at our garments. And then I kissed her, I don't know why. You could tell by the way her facial muscles contorted, that my show of affection had made her uncomfortable. "Tell me, then," she asked, "how is your father?" And I welcomed this opportunity to deliver Papi's message: "He is fine, Tía Lola. He asked me to please tell you how grateful he is for all that you've done for Pedrito and me. We'll be forever indebted to you, Tía Lola."

"You're such a flatterer! But you mustn't feel so obliged," she seemed affectionate. "I was happy to be able to help you. You see, I wanted to settle an old debt. Do you ... do you remember your grandpa Rodríguez?"

"No, Tía. I was just a baby when he died. Sorry. I don't remember him ... But we know he was your brother."

"Pedrito looks like him." She pinched his cheek. Poor kid.

"Yes. Pedro takes after Papi's side of the family."

"You, on the other hand ... " Now it was my turn to get a cheek attack. "You're like a young replica of your mother ... How old are you, dear?"

"I just turned fifteen, Tía Lola."

"You seem very mature for your age."

"Thank you, Tía ... Did you like the photos we sent you?"

"Yes, I did. You look pretty in all of them."

"The picture where Pedro and Mami and Papi and I are standing in an orchard, and you see a climbing plant behind us, covering a wrought iron window, and there's a lemon tree, that's a picture of our house."

Just then I noticed that Pedrito was covering his eyes with his hands. I nudged him, hoping he'd get the hint and bring his arms down. Which he did. "Go ahead, Pedro. Tell Tía Lola how grateful you are for her help. Tell her." He looked me in the eye and then, glancing at our aunt, he yelled, "Yes! But we're not going to stay here with her!" I could've strangled him! Tía Lola smiled. "He's right, Rosita," she said. "I am in no condition to be taking care of children. You'll be better off with Federico."

"Federico?"

"Yes. He's a loving man. He'll take good care of you."

"He will?"

"But you'll come and visit me from time to time, or I'll be very sad!"


Federico Rodríguez, my father's second cousin, had emigrated to Spain with Laura, his beautiful young wife, and with Laurita, his seven-year-old daughter. According to the story that Papi told, Federico had lived abroad for many years, mainly in the United States. When the revolution triumphed, he got excited about Fidel and returned to Cuba, to dive head first into the "process." But he didn't like what he saw and shortly after his return he tried to leave again for the United States. Only now the American government didn't want him because of his "history of communist activities." So Federico had no choice but to go to Spain, where he was welcome. "All of a sudden," Papi said, laughing, "this Cuban communist became a member of the Spanish Falange. From bolshevik to fascist!"

Federico had found out, through an imploring letter from Papi, that Pedrito and I would be arriving in Madrid, and that we'd be sent to the Casa de Campo if a relative other than Tía Lola didn't claim us. We'd be receiving a substantial monthly allowance from the United States, thanks to some arrangement Papi had made. Economically speaking we wouldn't be a burden; on the contrary.

Federico showed up at Tía Lola's house-museum the same day we arrived, prompted by Papi's implicit and tempting offer. He told us we could stay with him and his family for as long as it was necessary. But we'd have to help with the chores, and go to school and be good children.

He told us he was a salesman for a life insurance company. He had his own office in a tall building which was located in a throbbing area of Madrid, around La Cibeles. He didn't have a car because you didn't need one in this city; public transportation was cheap and reliable. He rented a plush flat, a *piso*, in a apartment building with a full-time porter, in one of the ritziest neighborhoods in town. Three bedrooms, bathroom with bidet, large kitchen, large dining area and a richly furnished living room with a brand new TV set. We could have our own bedroom. We'd be happy with him.

Federico (or rather, Tío Federico, the way he asked us to call him) didn't look at all like the people in our family. For one thing, he was light-complected. Short and stubby, he dressed like an office person, with a suit and a tie and a hat. Tío Federico was the personification of elegance, I thought. The most refined man I knew.

He seemed to like Aunt Lola and she seemed to be fond of him. They hugged a lot. "My beautiful lady," he called her, *mi linda dama*. And she just kept giggling and saying that flatterers were abundant in the Rodríguez family. "Such a family of compulsive flatterers!"

We'd get to see Tía Lola twice during our eight-month stay in Madrid, at Christmas and the day we left Spain to join our parents in California.

*   *   *

Mornings started to hurt me soon after we moved in with Tío Federico. Having to get up when everything was still pitch-black, feeling fearful, freezing. Dressing in silence. Drinking a cup of coffee with milk as fast as we could, then getting on the metro that would take us first to Pedro's school, then to mine.

My brother ended up going to a co-ed school in a poor barrio, around Lavapiés, far from where we lived. And I got into a more decent one in the Cuatro Caminos neighborhood.

As hard as I try, I can't remember anything I learned in my classes at that all-girl school, or any of the friends I made there. I do remember the songs that were popular, "Delilah," "Love is Blue," "Those Were the Days." And the ones that made me cry, "Guantanamera" and "Cuando salí de Cuba"; especially the latter, a song about loving and missing Cuba, about having left your heart buried there.

I remember the movies; my favorite, *The Time Machine* (dubbed in Castilian, of course). The fashion, those gorgeous bell-bottom pants and the platform leather boots. Wow! And I will never forget the entrance to the carpeted hallway of the building where we lived, Alcalá Street, number 100, corner of Goya Boulevard, across from the department store Galerías Preciado.

I remember going to Mass on Sundays, with the family, Federico saying that he didn't believe in God but that the church was a peaceful place and it was good for his daughter. I remember the gypsy women who sat by the subway door, holding their unkempt babies, begging. And my first impression of the metro, the image that stuck, the one that didn't get erased by the daily voyage through the entrails of the city. The walls of the underground lined with old, blind and tired men yelling incessantly, *¡PARA HOY! ¡LO-TERIA PARA HOY!* A depressing spectacle, those lottery vendors. Pedro and I woke up in the middle of the night one night, sweating and shivering, having had the same awful dream about those metro men.

We were walking down the stairs into the subway, wearing the heavy, unfashionable winter coats that Tío Federico had gotten for free at the Centro Cubano; long scarves throttling our necks more than keeping them warm; our hands imprisoned in thick wool gloves. The shouting and the peddling far away, *¡LOTERIA!*, like an echo, *¡LOTERIA PARA HOY!* Then the sounds getting unbearably audible, like an explosion of words, always the same words, *¡LOTERIA PARA HOY!* And we see them, fiendishly dragging their feet, touching the walls to guide themselves, pointing their canes at us. *¡LOTERIA!*

We trudge up the stairs but the door at the top is shut. There's no way out. We can't see the vendors anymore, it's dark, we can't see each other's faces, we can't see our own hands! But we hear them. Loud and clear and hurtful, their voices surround us, envelop us, accuse us, condemn us, FOR THE FROGS YOU STONED TO DEATH! FOR THE RATS YOU DECAPITATED! FOR THE LIZARDS YOU LEFT WITHOUT A TAIL! FOR THE CATS WHOSE BELLIES YOU CUT OPEN! FOR ALL YOUR CRIMES AND ALL YOUR SINS YOU SHALL PAY! YOU SHALL PAY!

We wanted to deny all those crimes we hadn't committed, we wanted to claim our innocence but we couldn't. We had become mute and blind, able to perceive only the sounds of their voices, YOU SHALL NEVER SEE YOUR PARENTS AGAIN! *¡LOTERIA!* YOU SHALL NEVER HAVE A FAMILY AGAIN! *¡LOTERIA PARA HOY!*

*       *       *

Pedro and Laurita fought like cats and dogs. I knew it was Laurita who started all the fights, but I just couldn't come out and accuse her, jeopardizing our stay with Tío Federico. We have to put up with her shit, I thought, it's for the best.

Laurita was a whining, self-centered and obnoxious human being. Pedro and I had this fantasy of ganging up on her and seques-
tering her and asking her parents for a million *pesetas* or they'd
never see the screaming bitch again. And since her parents wouldn't
pay up because they didn't have that kind of dough, we'd have no
choice but to silence the female rat forever.

"MAMI MAMI! PEDRITO PLAYED YOUR RECORDS
WHEN YOU WERE OUT! MAMI MAMI! YOUR TOM
JONES RECORDS! MAMI MAMI, ROSITA BROKE A GLASS!
PEDRITO WATCHED TV! MAMI MAMI, I'M A STUPID LIT-
TLE TURD, MAMI MAMI, I AM SUCH A BIG PILE OF CACA!
MAMI, PEDRITO'S MAKING FUN OF ME! MAMI MAMI!"

Oh how we hated her! And how we enjoyed plotting against her,
imagining her enduring the greatest suffering. We'd play the Game
of Pretending, and we would transform Laurita into a princess
trapped in an abandoned castle. We'd be her guards. Or her exe-
cutioners. We'd watch her rot away in the dungeon, drowning in
her own waste, frozen and starved.

Frozen and starved, I guess that's how we always felt in Madrid.
We had a hunger from years of rationing, a desperate need to feed
ourselves constantly. But there was never enough to eat at Tío Federico's. One meal a day and one serving, usually of white rice and
ground beef stew, *arroz con picadillo*, some bread, tomatoes and
coffee. Once in a great while we'd get to eat *palmeras*, a delicious
Spanish pastry. We loved the *patatas fritas*, deep-fried potato slices
fresh from the factory, and Federico would let us buy a bag from
time to time, never as frequently as we wanted to. He controlled
all of our money and would give us an allowance once a month.
He claimed we were costing him a bundle and that our father's
contribution wasn't nearly enough to cover all of our expenses. I
didn't know exactly how much money Papi was sending us, but I
knew it was a lot. Tío Federico was lying.

And so was Laurita. They were all lying. And we wanted to
silence their lies and their abuses. We wanted to be King Pedro
The Fierce and Queen Rosa the Fearless, and we longed for the
power to order the destruction of two despicable subjects named
Laurita the Ugly and Federico the Whitey ...


Welcome to the Fierce and Fearless Court! Vassals,

awaken the prisoner! Bring her to our feet, bring her!
MAMI MAMI PEDRO STOLE MY PENCIL! MAMI MAMI
HE'S A THIEF!
She doesn't know what awaits her, she has no idea.
MAMI MAMI ROSITA DIDN'T SWEEP THE KITCHEN!
SHE DIDN'T WASH THE DISHES! MAMI MAMI!
She can't imagine what she's in for!
MAMI MAMI!
We are going to amuse you, sweet princess. That's what
we're here for, isn't it? That's why we live in your
house, to entertain you.
MAMI!
Are you afraid? It's about time you felt fear. We know
it much too well. Fear is the worst thing you can feel,
the very worst.
MAMI!
Gag her! Swaddle her!
MAMI!
What should we do with her, Queen Rosa?
We should nourish our bodies with her flesh.
But what about her clothes?
Take them off.
Leave her in the raw?
Yes.
And then?
We'll eat her.
And can I do other things to her, Your Majesty?
Whatever you want, Pedro the Fierce. Go for it, have
your pleasure with The Loud Mouth, The Tattletale,
The Liar, The Imbecile, The Shit Head.
MAMI MAMI!
I know! We can cut out her tongue.
Yes, O Fearless Queen, but can I bite her tits first?
Yes.
MAMI!
Vassals, bring her to our feet, bring her! And shut her
up forever!
Will her parents guillotine us, Queen Rosa?

They'll guillotine us no matter what we do, Fierce King.

Pedro was twelve. "Almost a man," said Federico. "One of these days I'll have to take him around so that he learns about life." And he did, he took my brother "around." Pedrito came back with a thrillingly novel experience under his belt. And an incredible story to tell:

"We met up with this pretty lady at Tío Federico's office and then we went for a stroll at the Retiro and then we went to visit another lady, a fat one. The fat lady let us into her house and said Don't make any noise my husband is in the living room with some friends quietly please do it quietly. She looked at me. A kid? That's going to cost you more Don Federico. And I, I just wanted to take a big shit in my pants. I said to him Tío don't worry I'll just leave you don't have to pay more because of me. But Federico grabbed my arm and said You're staying! We went in and the pretty lady started to take her clothes off and she jumps naked into bed and tells me to kiss her Kiss me cutie kiss me don't you want to be with me? I throw myself on top of her I start to kiss her I move on top of her and she touches my thing and pulls it and pulls it and she says move this way and I move that way and she says try it this other way and I do what she tells me and she's getting impatient and I'm still thinking I want to take a shit and she says He can't get it up Federico he can't get it up! Tío Federico threw himself on top of her the same way I had and said Okay I'll take care of you baby. He tried and tried just like I had but something was wrong and she was pulling his white thing and making it red and pinching his white balls and acting impatient again and he was sweating like a pig and saying Keep trying baby keep trying. But he couldn't get it up either!! Afterward he told me that I had to shut up about what we'd done, not to tell anyone and much less Laura. He said he'd done me a great favor even if I didn't deserve it because I was such a retarded shithead."

*   *   *

Laura and I became friends. We talked. I could tell she enjoyed having me around the house, helping her. Laura had short

light-auburn hair. She was tall, svelte, and reminded me of Rosita
Fornés. One day I mentioned this resemblance to her and she
laughed, obviously pleased by my comment. "You look more like
her than I do," she said. "You even have the same name, ROSITA."
But Laura never called me Rosita. For her I was *Rosa*: "Rosa, dear,
sweep the kitchen for me. Rosa, please, set the table. Rosa, will
you do me a favor, sweetie, and go to the store for me and buy me
half a kilo of ground beef for the *picadillo*?" Rosa my dear. Rosa
my sweetie ... Rosa Rosa."

I asked Laura how she'd met Federico. "At a party," she mur-
mured, as if betraying an oath or revealing a long-kept secret. "Did
you date him for a long time?," I asked her, also in a whisper.
"One week." I couldn't believe it, "One week?!" "Yes, everyone
thought that the marriage wouldn't last," she paused, reveling in
the memory. "And here we are," she went on, "nine years later."
She must've been reading my mind. "Federico," she said, "he has
his defects. But he's a good husband."

But I couldn't understand how she could simply overlook his
defects. No, I wanted to tell her, he's *not* a good husband. He
cheats on you, he treats you like shit. Nine years later! Was she
under a spell or something?

We were having coffee in the kitchen, Laura, Laurita, Pedro
and I, and he walked in, bare-chested, holding up his shirt. "What
about this?" he threw the shirt in her face. "What about it?" she
asked, putting her coffee cup down on the table and inspecting the
shirt. "Is it dirty?" "No!" "Is it missing a button?" He poked
her head with his knuckles, "Yes! And you're missing a screw up
here!"

Laurita ran to her bedroom and shut the door. We did the
same, but we left our door ajar so we could watch the quarrel. We
were used to watching people fight. Fighting was the norm in our
house, whenever Papi got drunk. Our parents screamed at each
other, insulted each other. But, somehow I knew that they were
perfectly matched opponents. Mami wasn't the weaker one; in
fact, she seemed better prepared than Papi for matrimonial war.
Not Laura. Laura was a pitiful rival for Federico.

She went to her bedroom and brought out some thread, a needle
and a button. And as she sewed the button on the shirt she wept,

"You think I'm your slave!" He ordered her to hurry up, "If my clothes are not in order I can't go to work! Don't you understand that? And if I don't work nobody eats in this house. And you can't have your dresses and your boots. You have to help me! Don't you ever let this happen again!"

She handed him his shirt, trembling. "I wish I had never married you!" she wailed. He grabbed the shirt and pushed her. "Beautiful Laura from Vedado," he said as he got dressed, "the prettiest woman in Havana has become a decent and obedient wife. What's wrong with that?" She sat up. "Beautiful Laura from Vedado has become a decent and obedient maid," she cried. And she didn't say another word for days.

\*  \*  \*

Christmas morning I looked at myself in the mirror and realized that I had put on a few pounds. (And I had thought all along that we were being starved to death!) My brother was watching me as I observed my fuller figure. "Pedro," I asked him, "do you think I'm getting fat?" He just giggled and then spat out his insult. "Rosa the Fatso!" he yelled. "You're mean!" I said. "You asked me," he answered. Oh I wanted to slap him!

Madrid seemed festive. You'd hear lively Christmas songs, *villancicos*, about the Little Lord Jesus and the Virgin Mary and water that turns into wine and wine that turns into the blood of Christ; and *Sevillanas* and clapping and laughter everywhere you went. And I felt chic, attractive. I loved my cheap boots and my brown fake-leather overcoat, my fashionable sunglasses, the *gafas*; my hair, long for the first time in my life, and wavy. I had surely become a perfect combination of Marisol and Raquel Welch and Massiel and Rosita Fornés. My poise and my gestures had acquired a certain Spanish touch, *el toque*. Yes, I was bigger, but in all the right places. And yet my stupid brother, my tactless and cruel brother was telling me that I was fat. How insensitive!

He was the one who had come up with the idea of stealing food from the kitchen. Fat thief! "Sooner or later they'll find out," I warned him. "So?" he said. "When they ask us we'll just say that a spirit is sneaking into the kitchen at night and eating all the leftovers. The spirit of a man who died when he was hungry and now he has to come back and haunt people's kitchens pretending he can eat all he wants . . . " "But you see, Pedrito, that's not possible. Spirits have no tummies, they can't eat." "This one does! He's a glutton!" "A glutton called Pedro, yes! They won't believe your story for a second!" But the risk didn't stop him. He started stashing away in his school bag and later devouring anything he could find; feeding his face (and mine) every night in the middle of the night without ever getting caught. No wonder we were both becoming such lard butts!

"We're going to get to eat nougat today!" he announced Christmas morning, after insulting me with his "fatso" remark. "And juicy pork roast and gobs of greasy white rice and fried plantain and we're gonna celebrate the savior's birth and we can pray and we can make a special wish that we get to see our parents soon. No?"

He was trying to be nice, to make peace. But I was too upset and absorbed in my obese mirror reflection to be able to talk. My silence didn't stop Pedrito. He went on babbling.

"You know you're not really fatter you just look better you have a bigger butt only your butt you know it's gotten bigger maybe that means you're turning into a woman. No?"

Silence.

"And look at me I look just like the globe we had on our desk in Guantánamo round like an orange and red like a tomato look at my face I have these red cheeks like the Spanish guys I don't know and my belly has grown and my legs and my arms I guess I'm getting fat too. No?"

"Yes, you are."

"We don't have to go to school for many days it's Christmas vacation and we don't have to do homework and we can just stay home and we won't have to go out into the cold and we can just sleep all day and watch TV at night. No?"

"No."

"But then we'll have to go to Mass and go to confession and I don't want to confess anything today or tomorrow I just want to stay here with you Okay?"

"What is your problem with confession?"

"You look good with those pants and your hair long like that you know you look like those pretty Madrileñas who work in Galerías the ones who sell perfume they look so beautiful just like you Rosita."

"Don't change the subject! What problem do you have with going to confession?"

"Nothing. I know that we're supposed to be ready any time to take the sacred body of Christ what if all of a sudden you have an accident and you die and you hadn't gone to confession in a long time your soul would go straight to hell and you would burn there and ... "

"Pedro!"

"Yes?"

"Get to the point!"

"Okay."

"What is your point?"

"Well, when I go to confession now, I don't know what to tell the priest. I don't know what to tell him!"

"Tell him about your nightmares."

"But those are not sins!"

"Dreams can be considered sins, too."

"It was easier in Cuba."

"What was easier?"

"Confessing."

"Sure. You had a lot to say for yourself. You spent your days killing frogs and lizards and torturing cats and feeding live chickens to the pigs. You were a criminal!"

"I was not!"

"And now you have to be a little angel for your own good. It serves you right."

"I'm no angel!"

"Not today, anyway."

"Are you going to wear your boots today, Rosi?"

"Yes! Oh, Pedro, I love my boots!"

"Tía Laura doesn't have a pair as nice as yours."

"She has the ones made of real leather."

"But we can't afford anything real, right?"

"That's what Tío Federico says."

"I guess you're lucky that he bought you that pair, huh?"

"Yes. Lucky."

"How come girls didn't wear boots in Cuba?"

"They did. But only to work in the country."

"Hick boots. And you had to wear them! Rosita the Hick!"

"Yes, *chico*. I'm a hick girl from Guantánamo. *La Guajira*. The one who inspired the musical masterpiece of the century ... "

"Guantanamera ... "

"Guajira Guantanamera ... "

"Rosita, the skinniest girl in all of Madrid!"

"Flatterer!"

\* \* \*

I was washing the dishes and they were all watching TV. They loved TV, they watched it regularly every night from 7:00 to 11:00. Old American movies that sounded oddly Castilian, corny sitcoms, variety shows featuring the biggest Spanish and European stars of the moment: Massiel, Tom Jones, Karina, Petula Clark, Rita Pavone, Charles Aznavour, Salomé, Adamo, Mireille Mathieu, Marisol, Raphael.

I loved watching television, too, but I couldn't sit in front of the tube with the rest of the family until the dishes were done and the dining room floor was spotless. And then, when I got to sit down, I could be summoned by any of them during the commercial breaks, "Go get me a glass of water!" "Bring me a blanket!" "Make us all hot chocolate!" "Turn off the hallway lights!"

They were watching a wonderful show called *Los invasores*, a serial about extraterrestrials taking over the Earth, beings that acquired human form and mingled with Earthlings, invaders who would vanish into thin air if you shot a bullet into them. I loved that show, but that night I wasn't watching it. And neither was Tío Federico. He was right behind me, in the kitchen. He wanted something to drink, he said, and rubbed his body against mine as he opened the cupboard to get a glass. "This is such a small room, isn't it?" He was massaging my bottom with his erection. "Stop that, please," I pleaded, dropping the plates into the sink and making a racket. He pinched my breasts. "Don't do that," I begged him, "it hurts." But he was oblivious to my pain, driven only by his lust, touching me all over, my thighs, my hips, my butt, saying things like "I just wanna touch you. You're a pretty girl. A virgin. I like virgins."

I pushed him away, fought him, kicked him. "But you're my uncle!" I cried. "But I'm not," he responded, "I'm your father's second cousin. There's not much kinship between us. Let me love you. Let me have you. I have to have you." He pulled my hand down to his crotch. "Feel it," he moaned. I broke free from his grip. "They'll see us!" I wailed. "Laura could come in and see us!" But the danger and the risk didn't stop him. "I'll buy you all the clothes you want," he said, "and boots like the ones Laura has, the ones you like so much. And all the food you want, in nice restaurants. And you won't have to wash the dishes anymore."

I just couldn't believe he was molesting me only a few feet away from his wife, his daughter and my brother. What could I do to stop him? I grabbed a plate and dropped it on the floor. It broke, and the smashing sound worked like magic. Federico stopped, stepped back and left. Seconds later Laura was in the kitchen, "Another plate! You broke another plate! What do I have to do to get you to be careful!" She ordered me to go to my room. Which I did. I went there and cried.

That man who claimed to be my guardian and my protector, who was supposed to be my uncle, wanted to rape me. Who could I talk to? I sat down and wrote Mami and Papi a loaded letter. *Dear parents: This separation is becoming unbearable for us. We hate being alone and helpless. Why did you send us here?* I never mailed it, but writing it appeased me. What I really wanted to do was call them up and tell them that their baby Rosita was in the hands of a fiend. I wanted them to rescue me. But they were thousands of miles away. Only I could save myself. And I tried. And I did. I lured Federico into a trap. I teased him, I played his game of seduction. And then one morning, having driven him to overwhelming and unabated desire, I ditched school and showed up at his office. It was now or never, I thought. Confront the monster. Destroy it or perish under its paws.

He acted gallant and barely surprised; he didn't even ask me what I was doing there. He got up and shut the window as if by instinct, a mechanical action that had probably taken place many times before. Then he gave me a slobbering kiss that I received impassively, unmoved. He said he was glad to see me, that he'd been expecting me. He offered me a chair and I sat down. I had come to my senses, he explained. I had realized that he meant me no harm. And he was going to reward me handsomely.

His lascivious gawking was making me shiver. "There is nothing to fear, baby," he approached me. "I'll be gentle," he fondled me. "You'll enjoy it as much as I will," he sucked my breasts. "I'll make sure that you never forget this," he bit my nipples clumsily. "This is going to be the greatest moment of your life."

I got up, buttoned up my blouse and walked to the window; I peeked out. He was behind me, breathing heavily into my neck. I turned around to face him and pushed him away, gently. He laughed. "Let's stop playing," he demanded. "Let's make our nest," and he pointed to the couch. "I can't wait anymore." But

I didn't obey him; I walked to his desk and there I sat, moving papers and file folders out of my way.

"You take your clothes off first," I said. "I want to see your thing. I'm curious." He laughed again, and obliged me contentedly. He took off his shirt, his shoes, his pants, and I observed him. This was the most bizarre spectacle I had ever witnessed. That man stripping for me, giving me this show, that man grabbing his balls and his short fat penis and offering it all to me. He seemed so exposed and ridiculous. "Now it's your turn," he said. But I told him I wasn't ready. I drew near him and touched him. And just when I sensed he was about to rip my clothes off, I conjured up all the strength I was capable of exerting, moving my knee up between his legs, and hitting his balls hard one, two, three times.

He fell into the couch, bent by the pain, moaning and grunting and giving me lethal glances. I stood right in front of him, watching him as he reached down with both hands to cover his busted ex-macho testicles. I stood and watched him in silence, rejoicing in his suffering, avenged and fulfilled.

"If you ever touch me again," I said, heading for the door. "I'll tell Laura. I'll tell her about your whores. I'll tell her you're a liar and a pervert and a son-of-a-bitch. I'll tell the whole world about you. And then I'll kill you!"

I slammed the door behind me, convinced that Federico would never lay a finger on me again. And, of course, he never did.

*       *       *

I get these flashbacks now and then, of the people, the places, the food, the clothes, the music I experienced in Spain. And it all comes back through a cloud of freezing cold air, through the dense fog and the darkness we woke up to every day in Madrid.

Trying to get Pedro to be quiet in the morning was a chore. He was loud and expressive and he talked in order to assuage his apprehension and his fear, his feeling of loss. If he could talk things would be all right. I could sense that words for him were empowering: Speaking meant being alive.

"We're gonna buy *patatas* today and we're gonna put a lot of salt on them because Tío Federico never lets us put salt on them and we won't have to come home straight after you pick me up from school we can just go to the Retiro park and maybe even rent a boat and sail on the lake and we could write a letter to Papi and Mami and we could tell them about our adventure ... "

"Pedro, please be quiet. You're going to wake everybody up."

"It's so dark here and so cold it's always cold I don't like wearing that ugly coat the kids make fun of me at school they say I look like a beggar like a lottery vendor like an ugly blind man ... "

"You're not a beggar, so shut up!"

"I don't wanna go to school today I don't wanna be picked on I don't want the teachers to hit me and punish me and tell me that it's all my fault that I'm causing all the trouble."

"They hit you?"

"Don Manuel doesn't he's nice but don Romualdo does. He makes me stand against the blackboard and if I move he hits my back with his fist and pushes my face into the wall and squashes my nose and my mouth and then he pulls my ears and makes them burn."

"Does he punish everybody that way?"

"Everybody but he picks on me more. He has a long flat stick of wood that he uses to hit you and it burns like hell and it leaves the mark for a long time and then the other kids laugh at me during recess because they say You've been hit by the stick."

"Why does don Romualdo punish you kids so much?"

"Because we talk and ask questions and sometimes we throw papers and pieces of chalk around the room and because he's got a bad character he's always in a rotten mood."

"You won't have to go to that school for much longer."

"It's so cold here!"

"Put on your thermal underwear and wear your scarf and your coat and your gloves and you'll see that the cold won't get to you."

"It's like you're always inside a Frigidaire!"

"Jump up! Do it like me. Look! Jump! If you keep jumping you'll feel warm."

"Do you think we'll get a letter from Papi and Mami today?"

"Yes. With a big money order."

"And Tío Federico will keep all the money and he'll give us a couple of *pesetas* not even enough for one *palmera*."

"Be quiet, Pedro. He'll hear you."

"When are we getting out of here, Rosita?"

"Soon, little brother. Soon."

One Saturday morning in May, Federico said he had news for us. He asked us to get ready to go out to eat. He'd tell us the news over lunch. We obeyed. Apprehensive and not daring to ask him if the news was good or bad, we put on our coats and went out with him.

He took us to El Centro Cubano, a place where Cuban refugees could eat for free. "We're Cuban, no?" he asked, trying to justify our visit there. Officially we were refugees, he said. And we were entitled to a free plate of picadillo, white rice and guava paste, like the rest of the Cubans. The Spanish government was kind, he stated. Kind and magnanimous. This wasn't a rich country and yet it provided free food and clothes for the thousands of Cuban immigrants that had flooded the peninsula. "Franco is a generous man," he kept saying as we waited in line to get our food. "An exceptional man. He's brought Spain out of the ashes and made it prosperous, safe. Life is good here. Real good. There's order, progress."

"You'll be able to leave soon," he announced seconds after we'd started eating. "Nixon has just passed some law, that I can't remember what it's called, and thanks to that law all Cuban kids will be granted a visa so they can be reunited with their families in the United States." Pedro and I looked at each other, in disbelief, unable to say anything. Soothed by a sudden feeling of relief and safety, we held each other's hands and started crying.

Federico ordered us to eat our free food, which wasn't all that bad. "I hope," he said as if giving an order, "I hope you won't go and tell your parents a bunch of lies about the way we treated you. Always remember that you had a good life here with us. Thanks to me, you didn't go hungry and you didn't suffer the bitter cold. Always remember that."

Papi and Mami had been granted an entry visa to go to the United States; they had received the "exit telegram." They were claiming us from California, from our new home in Garden Shore. I shuddered, filled with terror, when I realized that after those eight months in Madrid, I had completely forgotten their faces.

# Four

GLASS WALLS. I will draw each ray of sunshine traversing the crystal-blue surface. I will not draw the beach, but the palm trees I will; they're essential. And the wind, I'll have to leave a trace of the wind ... *Leave him alone, please! Leave him alone!* The woman with braids and backpack who's left behind, in the distance, drawn forever ... *A home, a home where people love each other, is that too much to ask for?* The heat is vital, I'll draw it, too.

The traffic lights, the highway sign welcoming you to the city ... *I live with this fear that one day you'll go too far ...* The white Volkswagen chasing me, I'll draw it. The obese woman sunworshipping and swaying to Manilow's "Could It Be Magic." A skinny boy wearing green overalls and high tops. The brick façade, the red tile roof, the fruit stand, the pink and grey deco columns, the black wrought iron. Guantánamo Street, I'll draw it. Guantánamo Street leads to the sea.

An old man on his toy-house terrace, wearing a large beach hat and T-shirt, reading the paper. My sweat; my drops of sweat, I will draw them ... *What has Marito done to you?!* The stench of dead fish; the cool breeze that jolts me and revives me ... *What has he done?!* The voices of children who play by the shore; a hairless fleshy baby surrounded by his siblings ... *I will go crazy in this house!* Two ancient love birds searching for crabs in the sand, I will draw them. Invisible crabs that the ancient love birds won't be able to find ... *Crazy!*

The door of my house on Guantánamo Street, which one is it?

A new condo complex. Each splinter, each drop of cement, lumber falling, the sound of the saw, the nails that are being drawn in ... *No son of mine is gonna be a faggot!* The poster hanging inside one of the neighboring living rooms, I will draw it. Plants everywhere. The beanbag on the floor where later, this afternoon, a freckled young man will sit, the scaly skin of his nose and lips hurting ... *I won't have a faggot for a son! I'll kill him first!* He will consume a joint and will stroke his biceps, his thorax muscles and his thighs. *I swear I'll kill him!* Then he will run to the beach, to his freedom. I will draw his purple freckles, his shiny, sun-bleached

67

blondness ...

◇    ◇    ◇

Blue jeans torn at the knee; T-shirt with a hole on the left tit. Tall, slim; long hair. A song: *Falling down and down.* Barefooted, swift hands, bitten nails, fine white fingers sliding over record albums. *This need I feel ... This need I will fulfill.* Crowded studio; miniature stove. *Down and down.* Serpents hanging from the ceiling, writhing, vomiting green leaves and flowerpots. Wicker chair. Fleetwood Mac on the wall. Incense. From the waist up, naked. *Down ...*
    "Would you like some fudge?"
    "I can't stay for long."
    "Mmm. It's so creamy and sweet."
    "I'm not sure why I'm here."
    Self-conscious about my sideburns, my tight mauve-colored pants, my cotton short-sleeved shirt, unbuttoned. His murmur, "You don't need a reason to be here." *No reasons for love. No reason.* In the kitchen, a glass of orange juice, "Don't you want some? Here, have a sip." Wrapped in his blonde mane: I want to stay ...
    A towel around his waist and an order, "Clean yourself up!" My gratitude, eternal. But this was mutual, wasn't it? His pleasure as well as my pleasure. No need to be grateful. *No reason.*
    "Will you come back?!"
    "I don't know."

This painting of a little man in tight white pants, his hair bleached by the summer sunlight. Behind him, hardly visible, an older Frenchman of typically self-indulgent manners. Monsieur showers his little American *ami* with presents, worships him, calls him his young and talented *artiste.*
    Expensive dinners, grass, cocaine. Two cats and an aquarium. Shelves filled with Baudelaires and Mallarmés. The latest Charles Aznavour recordings.
    "Je t'aime," he says. And the little man pretends not to *comprendre.*

The little man's subtle watercolors and explosive canvasses crowd the Frenchman's livingroom, bedrooms and studio. "Je t'aime," he sings, "Je t'adore." Pretty pictures of a little man in tight white pants. Pictures without frames or walls. Pictures.

*Satyricon* at the Peninsula Theatre. Fragile beauty, Gidon. Blue-velvet, silky ringlets, milk-white skin. Gidon will give himself to the brave gladiator who fights for him and wins him. With his singing, his harp, his sweet tongue he will bestow a breath of life on the victorious warrior.

Gidon.

Tears are springing from your blue eyes, falling on my lips …

Violet rays, the waters of a stream. *Dove sei*? *Dove sono andato*? Crystalline violets and greens. *Perche non sono restato con me*? Grey clouds oblivious to this act. Oblivious to his pain. The powerful lord drowns him in kisses. His marble sex tears through the little one's entrails. Envelops him. Fuses with him.

In a room of mirrored walls an Irishman lights a candle and a cigarette. He listens to La Bassey who sings to him of diamonds in the greatest performance of her life. He collects ties and enjoys throwing parties for his company's executive clones. He cherishes an autographed photo of Richard Nixon, and he has pictures of Christ in every room of his mansion. He smokes and listens to Shirley Bassey.

In bed next to me, he places one hand behind his head, extending the other one along his body. A parody of sensuousness, an aborted male version of the *Naked Maja*. Later, the champagne cork will burst against the stucco ceiling. There will be wood in the hearth. A token-folkloric blanket laid out by the fireplace. And his lips on my sex.

I receive the champagne from his mouth and bite his cold tongue. A toast to our love. "This light becomes you," he says. And he makes a confession: He loves me. That is why he will let me sink my teeth into the skin of his back until the blood spurts out. "Do it gently," he begs. "But shove it," he demands, "and make me hurt." Gently? Then I should yank him off the floor, turn him on his back after I come. I should then smack him—gently?—and hit his face delicately, bathe him in champagne, let him drift into a warm and peaceful sleep in my arms.

Old, scratched-up records. The needle will get stuck on the last part of a song about diamonds, it happens every time. The next morning I will comb my hair under the red light of the bathroom, repulsed by the smell emanating from my clothes and my skin. Tired of performing.

◇    ◇    ◇

The host of the party forbids me to touch Jimmy. "Hands off!" he says. "Jimmy's a virgin. Forbidden fruit. Leave him alone!" Those are the rules.

The pitch-black host of the party considers himself a performance *artiste*. He gives himself away to Stevie Wonder and drowns me in saliva. He's a slick, anachronistic mannequin from the sixties, The Black Dandy. "Hands off!" He won't allow me to taint the boy's innocence. The white boy has a teacher already, a dark, green-eyed master.

Days later in my car with Jimmy, at a drive-in theatre watching a summer movie, a B-flick about a beach monster that hides under the sand and, when you least expect it, when you're carelessly strolling along, tanning or sipping a Coke—wham!—it surges and devours you.

Days later with Jimmy, a bowl of cereal and a glass of orange juice or black coffee.

"How do you make your living?"

"I paint."

"You sell your paintings?"

"Sometimes I do, once in a while."

"What else do you do?"

"A little bit of everything. I house-sit, I design interiors, I do commercial art, record covers, that sort of thing."

"Records?!"

"Yes, records."

We go to the beach and he dives, his body made of foam and algae. Playful and easily impressed, my Jimmy. Firm, round cheeks; the line of his spine, I draw it subtly. The splash of the water as he plunges in. His voice when he calls me, his trembling voice, yet undefined. *Jump*! I will see myself captured on the drawing pad, tickling him, or waiting to hand him a towel, when he's done swimming, or offer him a refreshment.

I dry him off and he laughs.

"What about the people? They're watching us."

"Who gives a fuck, my little one."

I bring my lips close to the nape of his neck and savor his skin, my tongue traveling down his spine, drinking in the salt of his pores. *Jump*! My pedestal, my bed of sponge. *Open the window and jump*!

The lubricant is cold at first touch but then it melts in my hands. "No," he says. But I insist. It will be painless, I assure him. His breath, his childish pouting. Lost little boy in my arms. The world at your feet, young man, I place it there for you, take it. Don't cry. Let's turn off the light and let me touch you. Let me draw you with my fingers.

On the phone with Mike. He's close by, in the area, and wants to see me. He had a bad cold but he's better now and ready for action. Am I? Am I ready?

Weeks earlier, he answers my ad. No ties or obligations, no questions and no claims. Pure service, nothing more, that's what I want. And that's what he has to offer. His servile voice on the phone, pleading and hoarse.

Recently out of the closet, ex-husband and ex-Dad, hungry commensal and punctual guest of the Bath House, Mike. Are we friends? Sure, why not. From a distance, from down below, your mouth on my cock, that kind of friend, yes. Is that a deal?

He tells me he hadn't forgotten my taste, that he had missed it. Panting still, he rests by my side. I tell him about Jimmy. *Il mio Gidon, fratellino*. An overdramatized confession: "I'm in love. In love like I've never been before, for the first time and for real ... His name is Jimmy. He's my angel, my little brother."

Mike laughs. "Incest is best," he says.

Thirty-first of December. Happy hour at The Laguna. The beach trail on motorcycle. Jimmy, sitting behind me, watches my friends sprawled like mermaids on the sand. The green-eyed Dandy cuts in front of us and performs a pirouette. "Pederast!" he shouts.

"What does that mean, peede ... what?" Jimmy wants to know. "Pederast. It means someone who likes to sleep with children." "But I am not a child!" he protests.

The music, always the music piercing my temples. Leaning against the bar, next to the jukebox, I listen. The melody travels down my throat, up my asshole, into my eyes, through my veins. It ignites the bushy line of golden hair that runs from my stomach to my crotch. It lives and lifts me, this music.

Joe behind the bar, an efficient octopus juggling glasses, ice-cubes, bottles, blenders, arms, hands, legs, cocks.

"I guess I'll have the usual, rum and Coke."

"And what about the kid?"

"He's not a kid."

"He sure looks like one."

"I'm old enough to drink!"

"Oh no you're not. What will it be then, a Coke?"

"Yes, a Coke for my baby."

Through the window, the ocean and the mist. He was tossing and turning last night. What could he have been dreaming about? I sat in the living room, hungry for thoughts. I've been thinking too much lately. And remembering. Jimmy called, "Come back to bed." I told him I'd be there in just a minute, that I wasn't sleepy. He said he wasn't sleepy either, that maybe we could just ... relax.

And now he's here, all smiles, bedazzled by his initiation rites. It's me I'm seeing, ages ago. The time I broke away. Low winter clouds, a regatta. Whales passing by, their bellies full of crayfish. Merry Christmas! *Feliz Navidad* at home with pork roast and black beans. How long ago was it?

Someone touches my ass. I push him, crush him. A grainy tongue licks my neck. The Black Dandy. Music again, from a spaceship. Five, four, three, two, one, zero! We take off, airy and anxious to explore the unknown.   Free at last, propelled, we're heading for the clouds.

But Jimmy drags me to a back room of screens where little mechanical men race down a merciless freeway. Some burst into pieces when they go off the road; some make it to the finish line.

"You wanna play?"

"No. You go ahead. I'll cheer for you when you win."

"I always win!"

"Prove it."

And he's right. He plays and wins. He plays and I listen ...

"We don't want your fucking war! We want love!"

"I went through all that hippie shit ...

We waved our flags and flaunted our long hair and we were so damned proud of our capacity for feeling ... "

"Peace love and rock-and-roll!"

"Desperate for peace and more than willing to kill the pigs to defend our freedom and our Dylan and our Joplin and our Morrison."

"And then one day you received your first big check."

"And you forgot all your peace-and-love shit."

"Guess I wasn't cut out to be a starving hippie heroine."

"Rebel without a cause."

"We had a cause!"

"Yeah. It was called Fucking."

"It was called Viet Nam!"

"I'm splitting, man. I ain't got no time for war stories."

"I must confess I'm a late bloomer."

"You could've fooled us, doctor."

"Let me guess. You didn't develop a taste for cocks until you were ... ten!"

"I was twenty-five."

"What?!"

"I was doing my residency in San Francisco ... "

"By mere coincidence, I'm sure."

"The gay residents had formed a group, sort of like a rap group that met once a month, and I was dying to go to one of their meetings ... "

"An obvious case of closet fever."

"Then I met this guy, another resident, and we hit it off right away and one day he asked me to go with him to the Gay Rap. I told him I really wasn't into that kind of thing ... "

"Liar!"

"But he said the Rap wasn't just for gays. Anyone needing the support of his professional community should go ... "

"So you went."

"So I went."

"And you got more than your fill of community support."

"The place was packed. And I saw people there that I would've never imagined ... "

"We certainly come in all shapes and colors, don't we?"

"The two men in charge of the discussion were talking about paranoia. 'We know for a fact,' one of them said, 'that here, among us, there are gays who haven't yet accepted their true nature. And we must help them. Those brothers live in terror and paranoia but they must know that there's no need to live that way; because we're willing to support them and guide them.' And then the other man got up and started moving through the room and yelling, 'Come out, brothers! Show us your real selves! We love you! Come out and join us!' "

"Oh dear, how threatening."

"I felt my blood pressure rising. I knew I'd throw up if that guy pointed his finger at me. But fortunately none of my other 'closet brothers' were coming forward, so the man stopped yelling and sat down."

"And you were closet-safe again."

"But not for long. A couple of days later the guy who had invited me to the meeting told me he wanted to sleep with me."

"And?"

"Did you?"

"What do you think?"

"The beginning of a beautiful friendship."

"The rest is queer history."

"If you care to hear my opinion, I think The Closet serves the same function as the Superego."

"Oh no. The Freudian Bitch is back!"

"Really. The Closet's a necessary evil, a device that restrains and tames the beast, the monster each faggot has inside."

"You mean the monster you like to have up your ass, right?"

"No, I was referring to the piece of meat that hangs between my legs, the one that came out defective in your case, darling."

Marty, the ex-Marine and ex-Castro dweller, runs across the dance floor making Tarzan noises. He talks about the art of Chain Reaction. "Chains are an excellent weapon," he explains, "in case of rape and besides, they augment the bulge." Standing on top of a table, he rolls down his pants and spreads his legs, displaying his neatly chained testicles. "Hurray! Encore! Encore!" we cry. But no. After the show, the ex-Marine retires with his bottle to a quiet corner of the room. There he will sulk, as usual, waiting for someone to *unchain* him good.

"I think our Castro sisters are all too much alike, I don't know, too mass-produced. What do you think?"

"Nothing wrong with having a common code."

"I don't wanna look like everybody else."

"Better than looking like you!"

"You fucking queer!"

"Queer Power, yes!

"Queers bash back!"

"We're reclaiming and subverting the word ... *Queer*."

"It's about time."

"The world is not ready for our type of subversion."

"It will be ready some day."

"The only thing I'm willing to reclaim is my virginity."

"He wants a miracle!"

"You guys don't like to face reality."

"Oh yeah? And what's reality?"

"For us? The plague."

"Speak for yourself."

"Haven't you heard? They say it's a gay disease."

"Well if it's gay, then it's all right by me."

"You stupid faggot!"

"Oh you're sooo butch. Go ahead and hit me, babe. You know I like it. Give it to me!"

"No! Suffer, bitch!"

"Oh good. Make me suffer. Don't hit me."

"They say you get it from butt-fucking."

"Get what?"

"The plague."

"That thing is a pervert!"

"Watch out behind you, boys!"

"What are we supposed to do, then?"

"There's always drugs and rock-and-roll!"

"What does the late-blooming doctor have to say about this so-called Gay Plague?"

"We don't know enough about it yet ... "

More coins for Jimmy's game? I have ten bucks left. I guess I'm poor this month. One more video race and that's it, kid. Then we'll go home. But I will stay behind him, playing for as long as he wants to play, watching over him, breathing down on him.

"What is that hard thing I feel?" he asks.

"Guess."

"Is it an umbrella?"

"No."

"Is it an airplane?"

"No."

"Is it a bridge?"

"Yes. It's a bridge."

"Can I cross it?"

"Yes, but be careful. You could fall."

"Are there alligators down below?"

"Yes. And they'll eat you."

"But you will save me, right?"

"I will."

"What if I die?"

"Then I will cry."

"You'll cry for me?"

"Yes, every day, for the rest of my life, I'll cry for you."

◇   ◇   ◇

Red luminescence and champagne. Happy New Year! Another song and the ship sails on. *Life is this danger, Love is this stranger*, sings the Punk Queen. Two young men on the dance floor, familiar faces. One summer on the cape, long ago, when I still thought of the past and the pain ...

In the bathroom, she pads my nose with cotton.

"You piece of shit!" He's right behind us. "Come here!" His fist into my mouth and my nose, again.

"You'll kill him! Leave him alone or you'll kill him!"
"I can't feel my lips, Mima!"
She wipes my face with a wet towel, "Look what he did to you, baby. Look at your face! Get dressed, my little one. Let's go to church ... "


"The most difficult and trying phase in our lives, the one you're going through now," *the arches up above, bright stained glass and virginal statues,* "you must master your desire, you must confront your physical self like a true and valiant Christian," *fireflies in the dark, a hunchbacked shadow lights a candle and kneels down,* "The Lord made you a man for a reason," *no reasons for love, no reason,* "One day you'll find a female companion and you'll be her guide, her source of strength and virtue," *infant god in his mother's arms,* "She's out there waiting for you already. She needs you," *grey clouds oblivious to my pain,* "Always be grateful to him," *oblivious to my fear,* "Always be grateful to him for having made you a man," *He tears through my insides,* "In the name of the Father," *He tears,* "the Son," *He tears,* "and the Holy Spirit, I absolve you."


The Cape Odyssey. A feather floats upstream. Two familiar faces and a punk song, *Life is this danger,* two bodies on the sand, drawn, captured by me forever. The hunky blonde in tight jeans wants change for the Ferry. But I'm broke, too. The feather floats and calls me. My feet on a ledge. His hand grabs my hand ...
"What are you doing?!"
"Let me go!"
"What were you trying to do?"
"I was gonna take a leak."
"Get down from there!"
"I was just gonna take a leak!"
"Down!"
Same old scenes. Sailboats reflected, lit-up yachts in the night full of stars. Any second now someone will come to get me. Like before, the way it used to be. He will come looking for me. He will find me. And he will take me home.

# Five

THE FIRST COUPLE of months in California I did nothing but bitch and ask that I be sent back to Spain. There was life there, good life. There were good-looking people who spoke pure Spanish and there was gorgeous music and crowded plazas. Here, in Garden Shore (a name that didn't fit the place at all), there were only cars, freeways and solitary houses. Nobody walked. The streets were always empty. How I detested that world. How I still detest it today, whenever I take a good look around me.

California was one enormous cemetery. Its inhabitants seemed ugly and haggard. Its music, *Baby baby baby I love you baby baby baby*, they called that unimaginative crap music. The weather was supposed to be the best on the entire globe. It was hot like Cuba's. Some rain, very little cold in the winter. And it would be easy for Papi to find employment there. Unfortunately not in an office, the way he would've liked to. But in a factory, where he could make lots of money right away. Yes, California was the promised land. Home away from home. Arcadia. But to me it became the vivid representation of hell.

⋆ ⋆ ⋆

Guess what I'm holding. What do you mean you can't tell? Records, you dope! Can't you see the faces on the covers? Look closely, *chico*. I know it's a super-old photo but try, look at it.

I found out through a Channel 35 commercial that there was a record store in Los Angeles, on Broadway, that sold Spanish music. The place, Discoteca Latina, was owned by a Cuban man, Señor Enrique, and most of his employees were Cuban. Reluctantly, Papi took me to Discoteca Latina one Saturday afternoon. He hated Los Angeles; he still does. He claimed that it was full of Mexican Indians and he hadn't come to the United States to mingle with an inferior race. That's why he tried to get our family located in Orange County, where there were more white people. We couldn't afford the ritzy places like Anaheim and Newport Beach, but Garden Shore—we were told by the Immigration authorities—was clean and moderately affluent, a predominantly middle-class city with a booming aircraft industry. It was far from the Mexican community of Santa Ana, and even further from downtown Los Angeles.

My record albums, yes. Papi complained the whole way to the music store. Why did I have to buy Spanish records, anyway? Weren't we in the United States? I should be studying English and listening to the American hits on the radio, not making him drive his '65 Rambler through those Indian-infested streets of the Angeleno metropolis. If anything happened to us, I'd be held responsible, he warned me. We'd risk our lives just to please me, the little lady, Baby Rosita. Why did I always have to have my way, he asked. Why did I consider myself so special?

I told him that I didn't consider myself special at all, that I was not a spoiled baby. My argument was simple: I hated American music and if I didn't find some way of entertaining myself, of alleviating my Cuban depressions, I'd surely commit suicide, as cut and dried as that. Suicide.

I bought, against his will, two Raphael's, one Massiel, one Karina, and one Marisol. "A fortune!" cried Papi. "Money I sweated for, money I bled for, wasted despicably on records!" Three of the albums turned out to be damaged; they were scratched and you could tell they were used or poorly manufactured. All of them, actually, were of the poorest quality. I was so broken-hearted. Papi drove me back to Discoteca Latina the next weekend, so we could return the damaged merchandise and get our money back. That's what you were supposed to do in America, he said; it was your right. But we were in for a not-so-American surprise.

"Impossible!" screamed one of the Cuban salesladies. "We don't take records back!" Papi was hyperventilating. "Well, you're gonna have to!" he wailed. But the lady was firm, "Don't blame us, blame your daughter! She was the one who ruined the records!" By now three other Cuban cows had shown up. You know the type: huge hips and butt, talcum-white skin, beady eyes heavily made-up, fake pearls and bracelets hanging from every limb, thinly disguised fuzz on the upper lip, the cow type. They were all telling Papi that if he didn't leave, he would have to deal with Mister Enrique himself, the owner, *El Dueño*. "Bring out that gangster! Tell him I wanna see him! Tell him I think he's a thief!"

Señor Enrique answered the call of duty, as was to be expected. He was predictably heavy-set, like his employees, had a black-bean belly and hairy arms, was balding and wore a *guayabera*. They just didn't make them more typical than that, I thought. (Oh, I guess he was missing the Havana cigar). "How dare you speak that way to these ladies? Have you no manners?" he asked like a true Cuban gentleman. "Gangsters!" responded Papi. Mister Henry turned to one of his employees, the one who had been dealing with my father. "What seems to be the reason for the complaint?" he inquired. "This man!" she spat out her words, "this man came in here claiming that our records are bad! The nerve!" "My money back!" Papi restated his case. "Or I'll burn down your filthy pigsty!"

And just as Papi grabbed Señor Enrique's neck, and just as Señor Enrique's face turned red like a tomato, and just as Papi moved his fist into Señor Enrique's nose, the choking man shouted, "Give him back every penny!" Papi let go of his neck, leaving the clearly visible marks of his fingers on it. "That's more like it," said my father. And Mister Henry, trembling, handed him the money, twenty-five bucks more or less. "Don't you ever come here again!" the owner admonished. "Don't worry," Papi told him as we headed for the door, "I don't do business with pigs!"

On our way home Papi and I reveled in a wonderful fantasy. We'd buy a can of gasoline, we'd go to Discoteca Latina at night, when the store was closed and there was no one inside, and we'd set the whole place on fire. But maybe that would be dangerous, we could get burned ourselves. Better yet: we'd go into the store during the day, wearing disguises so they wouldn't recognize us, and we'd hide a bomb under a stack of albums. We would time the mechanism so it would explode later that night, so that it wouldn't hurt anybody. Just as long as it left the entire rats' nest in ruins.

"*Coño*! They make me feel ashamed to be a Cuban!" Papi kept saying. "*Coño*! Ashamed!"

⋆   ⋆   ⋆

That picture was taken when I was a Freshman in high school. Can't you tell? The name of the school is right behind me, see it on the wall? GARDEN SHORE HIGH. And here's a picture of my friends; I took this one. That's Leticia and that's Marco and that's Ramón and that's Luisita. The cute guy on the left, that's Francisco. He sort of had the hots for me. No, he wasn't my boyfriend. And I didn't have a girlfriend either! Are you kidding? I was totally and pathetically repressed in those days.

God, I was bored to tears with life in the great North! The world seemed flat and predictable, nothing moved me. No, not even gorgeous blonde Gringas or the prospect of speaking the American language fluently. I was convinced that I had left my heart buried behind, on the island, just like the song said. *Cuando salí de Cuba ...*

I hated English and refused to speak it unless it was absolutely necessary. Papi used to get so pissed at me. Because, you see, I didn't always feel like translating his gross remarks when he was arguing with some clerk (which happened a lot). He'd tell me that I was stupid and lazy and that what the hell had he brought me to the North for and how did I expect to get ahead in life and get rich or catch a Gringo millionaire if I didn't "espeekee de eengleesh"?

My only source of happiness was the trips Mami and I took to downtown Los Angeles on Sundays to see old movies from Mexico at the Million Dollar Theatre. In that theatre that reeked of urine, I rediscovered, in ecstasy, handfuls of Mexican melodramas that took me right back to Cuba. Incredible, huh, that those dime-store stories and slapsticks featuring María Félix, Arturo de Córdoba, Sara García, Cantinflas, would make me long for Cuba. But they did. And I cried like a baby. Until one day when I got sick and tired of crying and decided not to go to the Million Dollar anymore. I need to stop living off memories the way my parents do, I said to myself. I began to see nostalgia as my enemy. And the images of my homeland that I carried inside as an obstacle for my success.

I stashed my Spanish albums away, my photos, my letters, my Cuban mementos in the closet. And I started to go to American movies with Pedro, because now I thought I was ready to understand them. The first American film I remember enjoying was *Valley of the Dolls*. The first American song I sang was "Aquarius." The first one I detested was "It's Your Thing." And the first American meal I remember savoring with gusto was a Sir Burger Supreme, with cheese. The rest I guess you could say is history.

Do you recognize me? Hard to believe that's me. Excellent polaroid shot, though, don't you think? That picture was taken right after I started high school. I was confused to the marrow. But fashionable. My hair dyed blonde, or rather what I thought was blonde (in reality a strange shade somewhere between red and brown, a barf-inducing color); wearing those dreadful bell-bottoms with the waist line below the hip, and that wide, scaly, worn-out leather belt, I was hot to trot.

The American students, compared to the ones in Madrid, seemed to me like people from another planet: tall, dead-white, distant, incomprehensible. Skinny girls with false eyelashes made of broom straw. Straight hair teased on top in the form of a nest, loose below, long and hanging as if all of a sudden there were a million greasy baby boas coming out of the high nest. Eyeshadow in blue, green, purple or all three colors smeared on their eyelids. Miniskirts that displayed long, feeble legs dressed in grey stockings. Platform shoes that forced them to drag themselves like war tanks.

Among the boys, needless to say, the blonde-boy type with T-shirts and pestilent tennis shoes predominated. The Koreans were gaining a reputation for being smart. Through a dirty trick of fate they had ended up first in Argentina and then in "America," so they spoke fluent Spanish with a Tango accent. There was also a species called Low-riders, drivers of Impalas, Chevrolets and Cadillacs at the level of asphalt. Mean-looking dudes who smoked marijuana and lived in Santa Ana. And the Blacks! How they had warned me at home to stay away from those Negroes! (Which I did, Heaven forbid.)

My GSH gang: The Colombian Leticia, who would one day become a flight attendant for Avianca and vanish into sidereal space. The Korean boy, Ramón (the name the Gauchos gave him), who would become a wealthy and stressed-out restaurateur. Marco the Ecuadorian, who would marry a Cheerleader and work in a factory all his life. Luisita the Cuban, whom I lusted after, today a mother of three and the resigned wife of a Marielito. Of all of them, I miss Francisco the most. Francisco El Mexicano.

Since I couldn't speak English, the school authorities "assigned" me to this Mexican guy, Francisco Valdés, from day one of my freshman year. He was an exemplary student, considering his "language handicap." I was told that he would help me with my classes and serve as my guide, until I felt ready to fend for myself. Whatever grades Francisco got (all of them Bs), I'd get, they informed me.

"Why are they doing this?" I asked Francisco. "Because," he said, amiably, smiling, "they don't know what to do with the recent arrivals."

And while we're on the subject: Those ESL classes! English as a Second Language. The darned classes didn't teach us a thing. They were taught by a thin, stooped old man who didn't speak a word of

Spanish, much less Korean. Mister "I-Don't-Know-What" would stand in front of us every morning and tell us jokes. I knew they were jokes because he laughed wholeheartedly at his own words. He talked and talked and cracked up and talked and once in a while he'd write a verb on the board, asking us to repeat: *I eat, you eat, he eats, she eats ...*

Francisco and I became accomplices in lunch-time escapades to the corner diner. I smoked my first and last cigarette with him. He was the only one with whom I spoke of my Cuban nostalgia. He listened. And he hardly ever talked about Guadalajara, his hometown, or about his absent family. I tried my first burrito and my first taco with Francisco. He used to tell me that Mexican cuisine was the most varied and flavorful in the whole world. Sure! How could he talk of variety and flavor when everything Mexican people ate was so spiced up that you could hardly taste anything but a raging fire? And besides, corn tortillas smelled of bats. No, I had never even seen a bat, but if I had, and if bats possessed a particular smell, it would definitely be the same smell as the tortillas. Little did I suspect at the time that I would eventually turn into a voracious and regular Taco Shell customer.

Francisco kissed me once, while we were walking to the diner. And I gave him the usual lines, you know: I liked him as a friend, not as a boyfriend. And I was too young to get involved with anyone, anyway. We drifted apart gradually, starting half-way through my freshman year. I was now excited by the prospect of being on my own, without an assigned classmate, and without a Latin clique to assuage my exile longings.

I had a know-it-all feeling about things when my sophomore year began. Sure of myself and determined to work for my own Bs, I was speaking perfectly accented broken California English, much to Papi's satisfaction. And I had decided to get the high school phase (without Prom and Grad night, please) out of the way as soon as possible so I could go to a good university, preferably one far from home. That was the American way: Move out to go to college. That's what most of my American classmates were planning to do. And I wanted to do as they did.

★   ★   ★

But you just don't do that kind of thing in a Cuban home, right? The kids don't go off and study somewhere far from the family. For my folks, even the thought of doing that was barbaric. I would only leave the house (this was implicitly understood by all members of the family) by the hand of my lawful-wedded husband.

As I'm sure you know, I had other plans.

I went to Cal State Garden Shore, a four-year school that was within driving distance of our house. And I lived at home until one day when I just couldn't stand it anymore, around the time I started going to the bars. (Can you guess why?) I managed to get the hell out of my Cuban nest without having to sell my soul to a man. How triumphant! In time, I'd be making enough dough to buy a condo in Seal Beach and move in with you-know-who, my "roommate."

I'm jumping ahead, I know. And you want the whole truthful story and nothing but the whole story, so help me Goddess. Okay, before I met Joan, the woman who would become my, how should I say it, lover? Before I met her I would do time in Management Science courses and seminars on theories of publicity. I was kind of thinking I'd become an accountant like Papi, or a business manager, or a publicity mogul.

Eventually I'd see the light and change my major to Spanish. Yes, terribly original. I would realize that business wasn't my bag and that school wasn't my cup of tea either. I wanted to be done with my education rapidly and easily, without having to endure too much suffering. School meant eventual freedom, but how great of a sacrifice was I willing to make for that freedom? Spanish seemed to be the most viable and accessible way out, considering I already spoke the language and I thought I had a knack for teaching, sort of like a vocation.

Those publicity and business courses I took came in handy years later, when I met Joan at a bar and she told me that she worked for La Agente, a Los Angeles firm that produced commercials for Channel 35 of the Spanish American Programming Network, otherwise known as SAP. She was a Gringa from Kansas City who spoke fluent Spanish (with a disgusting accent). My native tongue had been her minor at the Midwest University and she had traveled extensively through Mexico and South America. So I fed her this routine about my so-called interest in publicity and my passion for the art of selling. And she bought it.

In reality I didn't give a shit about business and I thought that publicity was simply legalized robbery. It was all crap as far as I was concerned, but what good would my true opinion do at such a crucial moment? There was Joan sipping her Bloody Mary and talking about production theories, sales dynamics, about forecasting and statistics, about the Hispanic buying power and about the Latino's consuming potential, and all I could think about was her tits.

Desire made my uterus hurt. And man was it hurting now, in that bar, in front of that Wiz-Of-Oz babe! Would she quench my feminine thirst? Would she sooth my aching lips, my inner burning? I couldn't feel the pain of love in my heart and that troubled me a bit. Love was supposed to hurt in the heart or it wasn't romantic, right?

Joan fell in love with me within a fairly short time and we embarked on a wild joy ride. (What a pathetically trite way to describe our amorous fucking!) Was I in love? No. I was in lust. I would never be able to love another woman again, I thought, the way I had loved Maritza.

Sorry, *chico*. I'm going off on a tangent again. Joan comes later (if I may be allowed the pun). First you must picture me taking Education courses in order to become *Maestra de Español*, and again bored out of my skull. I got my high school credentials from Cal State Garden Shore and landed a job at Orange High. I lasted there a year. I hated the loud-mouthed kids and the fights and the bureaucracy and the apathy and the long hours and the tedium of teaching Beginning Spanish day after day, hour after hour, to people who couldn't care less about that language. So I went back to Cal State for my Master's and got a job at the University of Orange, OU, teaching guess what? Spanish!

The university scene was definitely more exciting than high school. I didn't have to fight off the students and I got to teach some fun stuff like Latin American short stories. Nothing too advanced or in depth, you know, mainly third- and fourth-level classes. Most of the time I just taught Spanish One. The Department Chairman, Dr. Martin, wouldn't let an Instructor like me, who didn't have a Ph.D. (and who was a woman, to make matters worse), teach any of the more challenging upper division courses or the graduate seminars for the Master's degree.

I loved teaching Spanish One during my first two years at OU. But then, damn, Martin ruined it for me. How? Why? Elementary, my dear Mario: I was getting fantastic student evaluations, my enrollment was booming and I was acquiring a reputation for being the most exciting and real teacher in the department. And I was *too real* for our Argentine Chairman. He wanted grammar and drills and I was having my students play games. He wanted lectures on the Pluperfect and I was talking to my students about my preferences and desires, about my likes and dislikes, about my daily routine and about my latest travels, without ever using a word of English or explaining Spanish syntax.

Martin wanted the students to fill in the blank with the correct form of the verb, and instead I was having them tell me stories about themselves, linguistically limited but nonetheless intimate confessions about their habits, their fears, their joys, and their dreams. Martin favored accuracy over fluency and I was having my kids engage in Oral Activities without correcting their mistakes. They were having a ball and loving Spanish with their whole beings, not just with their heads.

I used a technique called Total Physical Response. No, it's not what you're thinking. It's a teaching technique I picked up in one of my Methods courses. For real! With TPR, you command the students to do certain things and they're supposed to obey you, responding only with a gesture. Don't make that horny face. It's all very professional. You start with parts of the body, *¡Tóquense los ojos!* (And they touch their eyes). *¡Tóquense la cabeza!* (And they touch their heads); then you go on to more complex commands like TAKE A LONG, WARM BATH AND SING "GUANTANAMERA" WHILE YOU SCRUB HARD ... MAKE A CUBAN SANDWICH ... MAKE A CUBA LIBRE ... OPEN THE WINDOW AND SCREAM AT THE TOP OF YOUR LUNGS I'M MAD AS HELL AND I'M NOT GONNA TAKE THE DR. MARTIN GRAMMAR SHIT ANYMORE! (All in Spanish, of course).

The big idea? Getting the students used to the new sounds without forcing them to produce them. They become children, you know, listening for a while and then speaking a broken form of Spanish and eventually saying more sophisticated stuff. Makes sense, doesn't it? And they don't have to know that the nouns *teta* and *cama* are of the feminine gender because they end in *a*; or that *pájaro* is masculine because it ends in *o*; or that *lo* and *la* are direct object pronouns, masculine and feminine pronouns respectively; as long as they can express their feelings and thoughts effectively in the target language.

Anyway, to make a long pedagogical story short, I was doing TPR in class one day when Old Fart Martin showed up in my classroom, pad and pen in hand, ready to evaluate me. Legally he should've announced the visit in advance, but Martin isn't known for going by the law. We were in the middle of a TPR routine when he walked in. Picture his face, ill at ease and totally red with a mixture of envy and surprise and lust as he watched my sexy Gringas touching their thighs (¡*los muslos!*), their arms (¡*los brazos!*), their tummies (¡*el estómago!*), their waists (¡*la cintura!*), and their plump behinds (¡*el trasero!*). Boys and girls, girls and girls, boys and boys massaging each other's shoulders, or pinching each other's cheeks (¡*un pellizco!*).

I improvised, on the spur of the moment, a whole gamut of activities which I felt were highly representative of my style (yes, I know I was digging my own grave, but I loved every minute of it): Among others, a small-group discussion in which the students had to describe their daily routines, preferably including personal and private acts in the description; and an impersonation game in which the students had to pretend they were famous people while the rest of the class guessed who they were by asking Yes-No questions: *Are you male? No. Are you old? No. Are you a beautiful woman? Yes. Do you have a husband? Yes. Are you a model? No. An actress? No.* And so on and so forth.

The most memorable impersonation? You'd never believe it. It was brilliantly performed by one of my girls in honor of our distinguished guest. She claimed to be a popular political leader who had been a whore in her youth and then an actress and then the wife of a nationalist ruler and who had been canonized after her death and who was known for a song she sang called "Don't Cry for Me, Buenos Aires."

Dr. Martin sat in a corner of the room trying hard not to be invisible, nervously scribbling curses against me on his yellow pad and throwing lethal glances at me whenever I gave him the chance (most of the time I tried to ignore him). He got up two minutes before the end of the hour and stormed out of the room. When I went to my office there was a memo from him waiting for me, taped on my door for all to see. Compared to his customary messages, which were flowery and verbose in the best Argentine tradition, this one was unusually direct and unadorned. *To: Señorita Rodríguez. From: Dr. Martin. Subject: Your Teaching Performance.*

Everyone in the department joked about *Los Memos de Martin* but feared them. A Martin Memorandum could describe something as insignificant as the new letterhead design for the departmental stationery (one of his first deeds as Chairman was to add definite articles to the department's name, so we became under his reign THE Department of THE Foreign Languages and THE Foreign Literatures). A Martin Memorandum could inform the faculty, as well, about the Chairman's recently revised review criteria for non-tenured faculty (which could mean catastrophic news to a lot of people). A memo could make you or break you. And this time a memo broke me. I would never get to teach my way again at OU.

In his office, he ordered me to sit down and he put the situation into the following terms: "Either you stop doing that reproachable, infantile, unprofessional and indecent type of teaching, or you're fired." I felt like telling him, All right you son of a bitch, if you want war I'll give you war. Either you stop giving me your power trip and get your nose out of my ass, or I'll go to the dean and the media with a list of every single student you've ever fucked!

But I didn't say anything. For some reason, I didn't feel like taking the little monster on. "Starting tomorrow you go back to the text," he continued, "and stop doing those humiliating pantomimes you make your students do. Is that clear?" I didn't say anything; I just sat there thinking some day somebody's gonna break this bastard's neck and justice will be exercised at last.

No matter what he said I would continue doing my thing in class, I thought. Let him have his pleasure. Let him be Bernarda Alba. Her index finger pointing to the floor, where Rosita kneels, imploring: "Please forgive me, Mother. I'll never do it again! I'll never make my students touch each other's genitals again!" And then, terrible words from the Terrible Mother, no mercy for Rosita the Old Maid: "Silence! I don't want tears under this roof! I want chastity and obedience!"

Little did I know that the Gaucho oppressor had an army of henchmen, *Los Espías de Martin*, who would invade my classes, disguised as students, and run with compromising tape recordings of my Oral Activities to the Padrino Argentino. "Instructor

Rodríguez is doing TPR again! She's showing pictures of naked people and describing those pictures in sordid detail to the students! She's still doing her communicative thing!"

Little did I know that Dr. Martin would make my life miserable, that he would haunt me, hunt me, determined as he was to mar my success and crush my creativity. Which he did. I would end up hating to walk into the classroom, disgusted at my own apathy and reproaching myself for not sticking up for my beliefs.

And too unmotivated to look for another job.

*   *   *

Funny. Now that the Goddess of Chronos summons me to talk about Joan, I don't know what else to say. I guess I could add that by the time I met her, I had already stopped fighting my "deviance." I had said to myself, Niña, your native island is Lesbos, not Cuba. Now what are you gonna do about it?

I had known quite a few women. I guess you could say I had experience. Joan didn't. She was new to the L.A. scene and to my scene. She was almost a closet case, a Virgin Lesbian. And I was more than willing to share with her my glorious pain that hurt so good. My love definitions.

Yes, I have to watch my ass and put on an act every time I leave my house. I need to eat and pay the mortgage, you know. I'm sure my folks suspect something, my Mami definitely. You've heard what they say about mothers, that they have a sixth sense. Mami's great, though; she doesn't bug me. None of my relatives bugs me too much, really. Except for my grandmother. She started to get on my case around the time I turned twenty-five. WHEN A WOMAN REACHES A CERTAIN AGE ... You know the routine.

I'd go see her and she'd harass me about the same old marriage thing. "Rosita, dear," she'd philosophize, "we are all going to be gone some day, your parents, me. Pedrito will have his own family to take care of and he won't be able to look after you. And you won't have anyone by your side when you're an old lady; no children, no grandchildren. You'll be like one of those lonely American women who end up in retirement homes. How sad, Rosita. I pray to the saints every day so that you don't have that kind of life when you're old."

Then, realizing that she wouldn't get a word out of me (I'd be biting my tongue), she'd concoct her own fantasy. "I know why you're so quiet. You have a boyfriend! And you don't want to tell us about him because you want to surprise us. I know you! You're just like me; I've always said so. You don't like to count your chickens before they hatch. You're waiting to make sure that this fellow's the one for you, that he's well under your spell, then you'll give us the good news."

Her haranguing was getting to be such a pain that I stopped going to see her. She called me up: "Rosi! What is the matter? Don't you love your grandma anymore?"

"Yes, Abuela, I love you."

"Why won't you come and see me, then?"

"Because I'm sick of your Cuban philosophy."

"Baby, I just want what's best for you."

"I know, Abuela."

"I want you to be happy."

"I tell you what, Abuela. I'll come by after work tomorrow and we'll talk about what's best for me."

"I can't wait to see you!"

I showed up at her house ready to end her matrimonial fantasies about me. I wouldn't be able to tell her the whole truth and nothing but the truth, but I would try to come pretty close to it.

"Look, Abuela," I said to her as I sipped her *cafecito*, "I don't have a boyfriend hidden anywhere and I have no intention of ever getting married or having children and grandchildren."

"Don't say that, *niña*!"

"I'm paying for a great retirement plan so that if I end up alone when I'm old, at least I'll have the money to pay for the best home in town."

"That sounds so sad."

"It's the way I want it!"

"How could you want the life of an old maid?"

"I don't live the life of an old maid!"

"Yes, you do. When a woman reaches a certain age ... "

"Old maids don't screw, Abuela. And I've had more sex in one week than you did in your entire life!"

"*Oye, niña*! What has happened to you? You never used to say such vulgar things."

"I never used to have a reason to!"

"This country corrupts people."

"I would've felt the same way if I'd stayed in Cuba, Abuela. It's not the country, it's me. It's what I want."

"I don't understand."

"You always say that I'm just like you and you're right, Abuela. We both like to be left alone."

"I have no choice. My husband died."

"You could be living with Papi and Mami."

"Yes, but ... "

"But instead you live in this apartment by yourself. You love your freedom."

"I have people I can call if I get sick. I have a daughter who looks after me."

"Good for you, Abuela."

"Who do you have, baby? Who takes care of you?"

"I take care of myself."

Pedro cracks nasty dyke and faggot jokes around me once in a while, hoping that maybe I'll open up and tell him, or that I'll defend my kind and betray my secret that way. But I have no intention of getting him or any of my relatives involved in my private affairs.

Fortunately my condo has two bedrooms and one of them is convincingly disguised as Joan's. When Papi, Mami and Abuela visit me once in a blue moon, I make them *cafecito*. If they ask about my so-called "roommate," I tell them she's fine, that I hardly ever see her because we have such different schedules. Then we talk about the smog, the traffic, or the latest hearsay about the Cuban condition. And thus the illusion endures.

# Six

THROUGH THE SLIDING door, a crack, the wind struggles to get in. A bag lady. The fingers, dirty nails, holding on mightily to the door handle. My fading face on the other side of the glass. This train that carries me, that takes me and takes me. And the sweltering air. And his voice on the phone this morning. His voice coming out of deep sleep. His surprise when I called him from the airport. "Hi. This is Mario. I'm here in New York. Do you want to see me? You're the reason I'm here ... "

One of the men wants to know if I'm from the island, if I'm a *Portorro*. Because he notices I have a suntan and I'm wearing shorts and I look happy. And I say "No, I'm from another island." But he doesn't believe me and he asks me where I want to go, he's the super. And he doesn't recognize the name I give him. Must be a new tenant; the name rings a bell, but he can't place it.

Restless. My Puerto Rican friend promised me he'd wait for me outside the building and he's not there. Could he be that dark stud peeking out of a window? No, my friend is not as dark and not as old. He's thin and well-built. That's not my friend up there.

At the corner he's waiting, at the corner. Run, I must run to his arms. Leave my luggage here, on the floor, the super will watch it. I must trust him. Is that him? Yes, that is my friend over there, the one watching the taxis, hoping to see me riding in one. But I don't trust the super and I drag the suitcase with me as I run. And I run. And I kiss him.

He's been waiting to welcome me to his beloved Harlem, to his run-down Upper Manhattan flat; wearing his everpresent *Puerto Rico Libre* T-shirt. His arms enfolding me, welcoming me this cloudy day to New York City. *Bienvenido.*

97

Inescapable noise, the noise of music. The salsa rhythms numb me. Total bombardment. He guides me through the ramshackle door, through a hallway where rubble piles up, where a black girl smiles and her mother orders her, screaming, to get back home.

The elevator takes forever and it'll stop on every floor even if no one calls it and it'll smell like everything else in this place, a mixture of fried, rancid food, old sweat and urine.

The super behind us, scowling. "Listen here," he says, addressing my friend. "You don't seem familiar to me, are you a tenant? Do you own one of the apartments? I don't remember you at all. Are you supposed to be living here?"

My Puerto Rican friend responds, matter-of-fact: "I don't have to answer any of your questions, man. But I will, to put your mind at rest: I'm gonna be living in 5B for a while. For a long time, maybe. Okay? One of my Sugar Daddies owns the place; his name appears on your list. I'm his kept stud. You got that? I'm his macho whore. Now leave me alone! Can't you see I have a client?"

◇   ◇   ◇

He points to the soiled windowpane. "Notice that old lady there in that apartment?" he asks. "The one across from us. The lady sitting in her bedroom?" Yes, there's a lady in a rocking chair. "Sometimes," he says, "I get up in the middle of the night and I see her sitting there, doing nothing. Day and night, doing nothing . . . "

He stands facing me, as if facing an audience. "Notice the cat outside her window?" No, I respond. There's no cat there. "Look closer, look at the fire escape ladder." Yes, I see it now. "That cat," he explains like a philosopher, "that cat spends its days and nights just lying there. It doesn't catch mice, it doesn't fuck or get fucked, it just sits like a fixture, sleeping or awake, submerged in a cloud of total and complete inertia. If you try to pet it, you'll get its teeth and its claws; it'll eat you alive." He sits, weary and pensive. "That cat's a New York freak, man, like the lady inside; that cat's a New Yorker. A paradigmatic and full-time reject. Jealous of its space, of its own oblivion."

Grey and filthy, jaundiced eyes, stained teeth and arched back, the cat's prepared for war. I observe it and disturb its rest, capturing its dull feline death in my rum bottle, entrapping its image and bringing it close to me through the dense glass. The feisty New York freak becomes a pussycat, meowing and purring in my arms.

Let's make a toast to my arrival. To Mario, The Client. No, my Puerto Rican stud is not expensive. He only wants my heart. To our reunion. And why not, to our love ... EXTRA DRY, *KERICO*, WHITE PUERTO RICAN RUM, *KERICO*, THE PRIDE AND JOY OF SIX GENERATIONS OF PUERTO RICANS ... Two dark faces, two pearl-white smiles, a collar of blue seashells, transparent dresses, white wicker thrones, impeccable rose-colored tiles, foamy cushions, crystal cubes pregnant with nectar, lace hammocks, a kiss ...

I envy the cat's peaceful sleep. I want its secret. I'll walk down the ladder and touch it with my feet. I must try to awaken it. I'll kick it. But it won't bite and it won't move. I mustn't leave it behind, half-dead and forgotten. I'll pick it up and embrace it. Feed it milk and cheese and dead mice. Welcome it to the world of freaks.

⋄    ⋄    ⋄

Most places are owned by Greeks in this part of town. Greasy donuts at the Greek Café. And for lunch, the best pizza in the barrio, Pizza Inn. I will savor the pasta that he once praised, that he once promised I would savor, if I ever came to visit.

The fat man behind the counter smiles; he knows I'm not from here. I turn to my companion, my tour guide for a summer vacation in Latino Hell. He wanted me to be here, to share his world with him. He wanted me to paint it. So I came. No plans and no promises. Just my love. My body, too. And my hunger. My teeth sinking into the best gooey cheese pizza in town.

Does he really not mind the fact that I'm a Cuban worm, a traitor to the Revolution? Does he not mind that I don't give a fuck

about politics? My paintings and my life in Miami or California,
I tell him about it all, I open up to him. I am honest.

"*Cubano*, eh?"

"Yes."

"Good for you."

He plays the piano, he says, but he can't afford to rent one. He
likes to write music and poetry. Puerto Rican from Manhattan.
Or better yet: *Nuyorican*. Angry Face, I would always call him
Angry Face. He didn't like it, but that's the name I gave him
when we first met, and it stuck. The day I met him in Miami,
at the Latin American Cafeteria, hiding behind a bowl of black
bean soup. What was my Angry Face doing there? Starting the
Revolution within the dangerous innards of the monster?

No no no, I told him, I don't write poetry, I paint. Van Gogh,
Picasso, Dali, Andy Warhol, Frida Kahlo: my idols. No, I don't do
anything new or original. Pleasant landscapes, people and things
I've seen here and there. Decorative shit that you hang on an office
wall.

Yes, I should come to New York. Maybe I'll get a break there.
Dreams come true in the Big Apple.

◊   ◊   ◊

As if speed could be seen; it is invisible. As if speed could be
drawn and painted and recreated. Impossible. You feel it, you
sense it, you possess it inside, in your guts. It makes you vomit,
you fight it off, try to control it but it's all too fast, too fast.

This train under the river. How can it go this deep? This fast?

But I survive the ride because I know he's waiting for me out
there, in his apartment, Two hundred and Dickman, Upper Manhattan. He's listening to salsa music, the windows shut, staring at
the little plant, still green on top of the fridge; another freak survivor, that plant. And the loud Caribbean men will be hollering
downstairs, in the lobby, or at the corner, and their macho laughter
will reach him, and he will quiver with fearful lust and curiosity,
thinking himself one of those real men. Man of the house. Hair
on his chest, a gold medallion.

The women standing in their greasy kitchens wearing rusty
black pans on their heads. And the young men proudly displaying
their tattoos of naked whores dancing on the powerful young biceps. The studs will walk to the window and spit out. He and I

will watch them. He and I will admire their sexy vulgarity. And
I will tell him about the bathroom basin, which is clogged up and
falling apart. And he and I will talk about the good-for-nothing
super who doesn't fix shit. And we will name him Super-Soup,
Super-Caca, Su-Portorro, Super-Turd, In-Supertable.


An old apartment that I clean on Sundays. I like to listen to
music when I clean. I play his records: Willie Colón, Tony Croatto
and Lucecita.

He's a ghetto grade school teacher who dreams about being a
writer. He wants to make it big some day and bring about changes
with his writing, get people to think differently about the world.
But there's a lot of work to be done in these schools. *El Harlen*.
The kids need him.

Once in a while I buy him a chocolate milk shake; he's a chocoholic. We stroll through Central Park. Or we go to visit one of his
revolutionary friends, the *Independentistas*. Or he reads me his poetry, which I love but don't understand. We like to visit museums;
we both have a weakness for Chinese food, we eat it on a weekly
basis at the Cuban-Chinese dive down the street. On Sundays he
fixes breakfast for the two of us: scrambled eggs, French bread and
coffee with milk.

I paint when and if I feel like escaping my feline inertia. I
imagine myself in a loft with varnished wooden floors and wall-
size windows; a spacious and uncluttered studio with a stove, a
small refrigerator and a water heater. Nothing more. And my
paintings.

He gets home in the late afternoon after an hour on the subway, takes off his shoes and throws himself on the floor. He talks
endlessly about the lack of things at school, the lack of everything,
even good faith. About the Jews who own New York, who criticize
us Latinos for being disorganized and loud, inept and overjoyous,
inferior.

This apartment belongs to his ex-lover. That's not what he calls
him, Lover; he's too macho to admit that he had an *amante*. He
calls him *un tipo*. This dude who likes to give things away and
who gave him this place. A good and generous friend. He says
he learned a lot from his *tipo*; he admires and respects him. The
man taught him about revolution, capitalism, Marx, bourgeoisie,

Freud, mythologies, Hegel, repression, liberation, proletariat. His friend spoke of Freedom and History. And now his friend is gone forever.

Something tore inside, he says, embarrassed by the triteness of his statement. The world became a cold and hardened city after his friend's death. Life was suddenly this feeling of not knowing what to do-say-be-write next.

Walking down Dickman, smoking a joint, away from the world as he knew it, surrounded by sad and somber strangers who had nothing to say, he felt like a ghost. For the first time in his life, alone. For the first time needing to be honest with himself as he wrote about himself. For the first time willing to accept someone like me.

⋄    ⋄    ⋄

The dude wants money. Anything worth anything. He shows us his blade. I take out a couple of bills, my Puerto Rican lover snatches them from me, "Don't give him your money. Let him cut me, let him cut me, let him try!"

Three stabs into the air, I hit the creep in the stomach. I should run, says my lover, I should just run. But the creep corners me, his blade on my throat. His order: "Give me the money." My plea: "Give him the money!" His blade on my face, "Give me the money or I'll chop his head off!" My lover throws the bills on the floor, the dude pushes me down and orders me, "Pick it up!" Before he takes it and runs, he slashes my cheek.

My Puerto Rican lover stains his shirt with my blood. He touches my wound with a handkerchief that smells of him. "It's nothing," he says. "Don't be alarmed, he didn't cut deep." He caresses my aching cheek. "Yes, please. Make it better."

Red and green street neons shed their light on his shoulders and his naked chest. I feel dizzy; in my mouth a bitter taste of blood and alcohol. He kisses me reluctantly, but he will let me run my tongue down his arms, his neck; down the ecstasy line that passes through his belly button, that leads to his pubis and there it becomes a fragrant thicket, that ends on his throbbing erection.

He'll let me savor his thighs, lick the dense black ringlets on his legs. He'll let me seek and find, anxiously, the warmth and the taste of his balls, overflowing and tender, he'll let me drink from them. His prick belongs to me. He'll let me count each tiny vein, each tender wrinkle. He'll let it be my toy. Reddish brown, mushroom head. Baby pink tongue on his huge head. This is his offering. And now he's ready for mine. Some fun. Yes, he's right. It'll keep my mind off the pain ...

◇    ◇    ◇

The girdle, the stockings, the high heels. Moist lips. The eyelashes longer, longer. The forehead ample and clear and the waist-length amber hair waving and writhing. In front of the mirror: *I belong to a famous New York tailor.* My chin barely touching the left shoulder; close-up of my bare back, turning my head to face him. The arms ahead of me, splayed, and then the hands reposing on my thighs. Daring and alluring, provocative: *I am his private mannequin.*

I hear the overture, wet my lips with the tip of my tongue and clear my throat, let my voice be an echo. What should I be thinking right before I go on stage? What should I feel? Should I lean against the wall of my dressing room? Should I close my eyes and sing, *Lover, if only I had a heart*? The hips swaying subtly. But the shoulders moving in frenzy, throwing my head back. That's it: I am the latest cry. Moving down slowly when I hear the trumpets; rocking my body in place, down and down. One last time: *But mannequins don't have a heart ...*

# Seven

MARIO: THOSE POTATOES you're peeling, Señora Rosa, look good enough to eat raw.

ROSA: Why, Don Mario, these are not potatoes.

MARIO: They're not?

ROSA: No. They're bull testicles.

MARIO: Ay! Now I'm really hungry!

ROSA: Do something then, *chico*.

MARIO: Such as?

ROSA: Slice the tomatoes.

MARIO: With pleasure.

ROSA: We're gonna have a healthy meal today.

MARIO: For a change.

ROSA: Butterless mashed potatoes, mixed salad with low-calorie dressing and multiple-grain-multiple-vitamin bread sticks with cholesterol-free margarine.

MARIO: And for dessert, low-fat frozen yogurt.

ROSA: No fried plantain and no *picadillo*.

MARIO: Not for us; we're a unique breed of *Cubanos*.

ROSA: Cuban hyphen Americans, please.

MARIO: Cuban hymen Americans, you mean.

ROSA: Here. Have a bread stick. That'll tide you over till dinner time.

MARIO: You sound repulsively motherly, Lovely Rosa.

ROSA: Tough.

MARIO: Actually, I'm not in the mood for eating yet.

ROSA: And what are you in the mood for, sweetheart?

MARIO: For truth.

ROSA: *Coño*.

MARIO: Oh yes.

ROSA: Okay. I'll give you some truth. Look at this memo.

MARIO: A Martin Memorandum?

ROSA: Deactivation!

MARIO: Excuse me?

ROSA: It's the latest feat of the Curriculum Committee.

MARIO: A committee that has only one member, I suspect.

ROSA: Doctor Martin!

MARIO: Deactivation!

107

ROSA: The Great Administrator is going around slashing courses, destroying the work that took blood, sweat and tears to build!

MARIO: Yes, indeed. The memo states it clearly. COURSES THAT HAVEN'T BEEN TAUGHT IN THE LAST TWO YEARS WILL BE DEACTIVATED.

ROSA: Enough truth. Let's have a Cuba Libre.

MARIO: How a propos.

ROSA: Enter my bar and play the shrink for me, Don Mario.

MARIO: Great! I've always wanted to do a shrink scene.

ROSA: To be or not to be deactivated, that is the question!

MARIO: But we don't want to be deactivated! We want to live!

ROSA: Put on my Matador hat!

MARIO: Oh yes! The red velvet hat!

ROSA: Your right hand on your chest, moving forward and upward, impetuously. Give it to me, Matador!

MARIO: Get out of my way, you stupid bull!

ROSA: *Olé!*

MARIO: If you take my courses you'll have to take me!

ROSA: Martin's not your type, baby.

MARIO: I'll go down fighting. Like a man!

ROSA: Fat chance.

MARIO: Hey, speak for yourself.

ROSA: Don't make your audience wait!

MARIO: Ah yes. I enter the bar wearing sunglasses and white cotton pants.

ROSA: You're a fat and aging version of Don Johnson.

MARIO: And I'm too old and too cynical, even if I dress hip and have a teenage wife, to believe that any teaching methodology can solve our problems, right?

ROSA: Right on.

MARIO: I'm Dr. Cotton Pants, the Ruler's personal advisor.

ROSA: You're in charge of his army!

MARIO: What we need to do is what we know how to do best. Teach! There's nothing wrong with using the same exams that we've been using for the last three decades. Who dares say there's anything wrong with that?

ROSA: Applause! Applause!

MARIO: Forget the communicative-talkative-putative-infantile new methods. We're not clowns. We're professionals!

ROSA: Viva! Eureka!

MARIO: I know what I'm doing. I'm not just your average horny little teacher. I am a doctor of philosophy. I wrote a dissertation, damn it! Look at me. You better believe me. I am a Doctor!

ROSA: Here, have a sip of Free Cuba. You've earned it.

MARIO: Cheers!

*

ROSA: An upbeat tango ... You hear it?

MARIO: Punk tango, yes.

ROSA: The perfect musical theme ...

MARIO: Indeed. Enter the Latin American Dictator!

ROSA: According to a popular academic legend, once upon a time there was this humble and dedicated literature professor who used to fight for all the noble causes at the University of Orange ...

MARIO: Mmmm ... I love a hero.

ROSA: This Argentine professor, whom we shall call Steel Martin, was a self-proclaimed socialist-humanist who stood up for the underdogs ...

MARIO: Another sexy Zorro!

ROSA: He was the only one valiant enough to challenge the powerful Gringo chairman at departmental meetings, denouncing his dictatorial ways, his lack of democratic decency, his archaic worldview ...

MARIO: Steel was made of steel!

ROSA: Yes. Steel was made of steel when it came to criticizing hierarchies, sites of power, exploitation ...

MARIO: And he didn't get fired?

ROSA: No. Because he published. In the eyes of the Overseeing Administrators, Dr. Martin was a brilliant scholar, known internationally as an authority on Argentina's Gaucho culture masterpiece, the epic poem *Martín Fierro*.

MARIO:The Gringo dictator couldn't touch him.

ROSA: His courses would never be deactivated ... But then.

MARIO: Oh then.

ROSA: The winds of time swept through the Vitamin C Institution, bringing new faces, fresh ideas, radical theories and revolutionary teaching methodologies to the little Foreign Languages Department.

MARIO: It's a new era!

ROSA: The powerful Gringo chairman retired to a condo in Cancún and his old boys network started to dissolve.

MARIO: And little did anyone suspect that the socialist radical Martin was lurking in the dark.

ROSA: Yes. Waiting to take a big bite out of the chair.

MARIO: Behind the humanitarian Gaucho stood a despot and a power-hungry monster.

ROSA: No sooner had the Gringo stepped down from the throne, than Tiny Martin started moving his books into the chairman's office. And not long after taking possession of the Gringo's court, he formed an alliance with Dr. Cotton Pants, another Argentinean professor.

MARIO: The Neo-Tango Alliance!

ROSA: Dr. Martin's first great deed was the deactivation of certain "bad" words ...

MARIO: Such as?

ROSA: Structuralism, discourse, semiotics, new historicism, culture crack, dialogism, parody, reader-response, deconstruction, postmodernism, gender construct, feminism, transculturation and empowerment.

MARIO: Dangerous words indeed. What do they mean?

ROSA: When it was time to choose a textbook for the elementary courses, he put together a selection committee and then vetoed the committee's decision because, he claimed, the book they had chosen was too "fragmented."

MARIO: Only *whole* and *holy* texts are allowed in Martin's court!

ROSA: So he forced on us a book he had used when he was a teaching assistant, back in the beginning of Argentine pedagogical history. Solid grammar exercises and drills, that's what foreign language pedagogy was about, according to him.

MARIO: Don't anyone dare propose anything else!

ROSA: He overloaded all the classes and gave two extra courses a semester to each faculty member. He decided what upper division courses and graduate seminars would be taught, at what time, where and by whom. It was also his decision who would go on sabbatical and who should apply for a grant.

MARIO: History repeats itself.

ROSA: Then he wrote up a proposal that fortunately never got funded, in which he asked for the department to be turned

into a center for Gaucho Epic Poetry Studies. But worst
of all: he started sleeping with his students.

MARIO: Poor, poor girls.

ROSA: They would enroll in his courses cherishing hopes about
reading Regionalist poetry and Magical Realist novels, eager and willing to taste the fruit of Hispanic knowledge ...

MARIO: Plump rosy Gringo apples that the cacique would devour
in his hours of lechery.

ROSA: Ouch!

MARIO: Did he ever try to take a bite out of the rosy Rosi?

ROSA: Yes. But my apple had a worm!

MARIO: Is that why you've never gotten a raise?

ROSA: Elementary, my dear Mario.

MARIO: Look at me!

ROSA: Yes, yes! You are the Great Steel Martin! Yes. Pace the
room with your butt sticking out, like a dwarf in uncomfortable shoes. You're a mean dude!

MARIO: I am so hot, Che. *Vos lo sabés.* So hot. I publish in
the most prestigious journals and I'm quoted. I have produced a dozen books and hundreds of reviews. I am the
greatest!

ROSA: Subjects, applaud!

MARIO: Long Live Steel Martin! The legendary son of Martín
Fierro!

ROSA: Subjects, lift him! And carry him across campus!

*

MARIO: I need another drink.

ROSA: So do I.

MARIO: Let's get back to you now, Lovely Rosa.

ROSA: Back to me? That's no fun.

MARIO: It can be.

ROSA: The shrink scene is over, Marito.

MARIO: Not yet. Not until you answer a couple of questions.

ROSA: Okay. Shoot.

MARIO: Tell me, baby, what do you really teach your students?

ROSA: The Spanish language, of course.

MARIO: Hah!

ROSA: That's the truth.

MARIO: Hah!

ROSA: Okay, okay, you guessed my secret. I send them sub-
liminal messages of polymorphous perverse sexuality that
are magically embedded in my Comprehensible Input. I
lower their Affective Filter and teach them the forbidden
pleasure of Total Physical Response. I allow for them to
go through a Natural Order, proceed at their own pace. I
never rush them. I give them the time to acquire and I
let them produce for me when they're ready. And most of
all, I show them pictures.

MARIO: Yes, but your "Total Physical Response" is only part of
the truth.

ROSA: What are you getting at?

MARIO: You're also a closet Lit Freak.

ROSA: That's it, *coño*! That's the source of all my stress. I want
to teach literature and Martin won't let me!

MARIO: I knew it!

ROSA: But I do, anyway. Whenever I get the chance.

MARIO: Secretly, Rosa Rodríguez becomes the clandestine literary
critic!

ROSA: Yes. I talk to my babies about houses inhabited by spirits.
About gypsies, flying carpets, yellow butterflies. About
banana companies and forbidden jungles, about eternal
civil wars, about hopscotch and labyrinths, about songs
that break your heart and about deserted islands ...

MARIO: And when all the words are said and all the stories told,
you go back to your Ivory Condo ...

ROSA: Yes. And I dream.

MARIO: What do you dream about?

ROSA: The past.

MARIO: How unoriginal, sweetheart.

ROSA: I have no problems with my lack of originality.

MARIO: I do.

ROSA: I know.

MARIO: What other truths about yourself can you share with us
today, Señora Profesora?

ROSA: I could tell you that I hate faculty meetings, that I don't give
a shit about who won the football game, that I couldn't
care less if the Department was authorized to search for
a position in Chinese; if the university got a sizeable do-
nation from a filthy-rich businessman for the School of
Engineering; if the faculty would now be able to have free

coffee, access to a new computer, or the opportunity to sign a mural-sized Christmas card for Steel Martin ...

MARIO: I wanna wish you a merry Christmas! ...

ROSA: And most of all I hate the gossip, *coño*!

MARIO: Ay, *niña*, but gossip is so fun.

ROSA: Not when it's about you.

MARIO: Juicy subject.

ROSA: They hang affairs on me, affairs with men!

MARIO: Wonderful! What are you complaining about?

ROSA: They say that I'm a Prima Donna. And a slut.

MARIO: Welcome to the club, *prima*.

ROSA: Because they can't figure me out. I don't play their games.

MARIO: Oh yes, you're above all that filth. You have no tolerance or patience for human nature. You're lovely Rosa.

ROSA: I won't kiss ass!

MARIO: Yes, baby, I know. Roses and asses don't blend well.

ROSA: Whose side are you on anyway?

MARIO: On yours. Always.

ROSA: You could've fooled me!

MARIO: Is it possible, Professor Rodríguez, that you just don't belong in a university?

ROSA: It is possible.

MARIO: Could it also be, *maestra*, that you've got to make a decision about what the fuck you want to do with your life?

ROSA: Sooner or later, yes.

MARIO: The sooner the better.

ROSA: I'm hungry. Let's eat.

MARIO: Finally!

$\star$  $\star$  $\star$

My eyes closed, I imagine her skin. Soft? Warm? And my lips on her breasts. She's wearing a tight skirt and stockings. My hands under her skirt. The edge of the stockings, where the fabric ends and the skin begins. The dampness, the smell. A saline smell. Playing with her pubic hair, then drinking that slippery dampness. Drinking eternally, to the point of satiation, as if each drop of love were the last drop.

She stares at me, thinking I'm asleep. She touches the tepid surface of my breasts. I spread my legs and the throbbing sensation begins. She inserts her finger, leaving it there, moving it lightly, inundating me with images of blades that cut through thick ice blocks, like skates, making the tiny chips of frozen water jump and bathe me. My hands are cups overflowing with her burning skin. Her nipples, hard and pointed. She laces my waist with her arms and brings out her finger, leaving me lifeless for a split-second.

Yes, baby, I am wet. But she wants more. And so do I. Two, three fingers inside, rubbing in circles, stopping at perfectly synchronized intervals; around and deep, the rhythm of her fingers and her tongue. Ants in my veins. I have no arms no legs no heart no lungs no face. An all-consuming kiss consuming all of me. I am her tongue inside, the movement of her hands, this river that grows. Where she swims. I am her.

★   ★   ★

Joan tried, unsuccessfully, to make a meat-and-potatoes kind of gal out of me. She detested my boisterous, melodramatic and "dishonest" Spanish music (Joan is into "honest" music). She tried to turn me on to Emmy Lou Harris and Linda Ronstadt (long before Linda put on her Mariachi hat). She taught me the secrets of the American Lexicon, words I'd never heard before and that I thought I was incapable of using, like *discombobulated*: "Not tonight, honey. I feel discombobulated."

She was lovingly condescending about my accent and set out to give me diction lessons on a regular basis. She claimed that Cuban cuisine was unbearably delicious but totally unhealthy. She got me to try, for about a month, a high-fiber, cholesterol-free diet. She showed me the wonders of camping and hiking and mountain climbing. (I still can't believe that she loves to leave the comfort of the home for the discomfort of the outdoors, calling her outing a "vacation.") She tried to make me see that there was more to this great country than Los Angeles, that the Midwest was real, that there were people and families and snow storms and tornadoes and beautiful autumns and springs out there. She tried, again unsuccessfully, to get me to visit her beloved Land of Oz. She tried.

Meanwhile, I was feeling diluted, lost in a labyrinth of freeways and malls. Secretly feeding myself juicy Sir Burger Supremes, greasy French fries. Sick of Joan's slogans and her high-budget commercials for La Agente. Sick of the costly artifacts that she produced. Her power trip, a team of people under her: writers, light technicians, cameramen, makeup artists, musicians, choreographers, sound specialists, budget advisors, and the big Latino stars who sell the product (and themselves) to the Hispanic masses. (Sorry, no names mentioned; we must avoid a lawsuit at all costs.)

A small sampling of Joan's *key* lexical items: *Consumer Potential, Risk Margin, Sale.* Her smiles and her flirting disguise a secret agenda. She displays her charts, her compelling statistics in order to prove the pressing necessity of reaching the Hispanic consumer: a gold mine, an untapped well. Her masterpiece TV commercials to date:

Delicious chunks of Pollo Bobo Chicken, TRY IT! EAT IT WITH TORTILLAS AND REFRIED BEANS AND YOU WILL NEVER RUN TO THE COLONEL AGAIN!

Thirst-quenching and delightfully sweet Pop Cola, DRINK IT, LATINO! CATCH THE NEW ONDA! INCORPORATE YOURSELF, LATINO! BE PART OF THE NEW GRINGO CONSTELLATION!

Spanish-language billboards have sprung up all over the city. What more proof do we need of our important contribution to the culture of this great and fertile land? We've made it. We have arrived.

Joan's biggest client: Spanish American Programming Network (SAP!), which is owned by a Mexican mafioso. Ten soap operas a day, with lots of crying and dime-store hysteria, adultery, cheap erotica, prepotent men, insane, devious women and deceptively naive young maidens. Trash.

Trash, claims Joan, is unfortunately all that the Hispanic masses can relate to: maudlin, unrealistic and overacted little dramas. Why, it has been proven statistically! Quality programming gets low ratings. The French-made series about famous artists, *La vida de un artista*, for example, got cancelled after the third episode (which happened to be the one about Frida Kahlo): no one was watching the show!

Trash, according to the charts, is the only thing we can digest, the only hook that lures us to the tube so that we swallow tons of commercials and buy every piece of junk advertised so Joan keeps selling her artsy-craftsy lies and the Mexican magnate can continue making his millions. *Coño*!

Once a week Joan's boss comes around to pester her. He reminds her that she went over budget again, that she's handling the
personnel inefficiently, that SAP requires more attention, that she
asks too many questions and doesn't familiarize herself enough
with the company's assets and limitations; that her slogans are
becoming arty and verbose. That she's not responding properly,
with the right amount of kiss-ass and coquettishness, to the com-
pliments, remarks and demands of the "older accounts." Maybe
she's not cut out to be the Hispanic liaison after all, the Spanish-
language producer. Maybe she's totally wrong for the job. But is
she?

What is a Gringa from the Emerald City doing in the City of
Angels, anyway? How did she end up selling Pop Cola and pizza
and diapers and cereal and Bobo Chicken and the American Dream
to the masses of undocumented workers and working-class and
middle-class Latinos who inhabit the West Coast metropolis? How
did she manage? How was such an ultimate irony possible?

Joan tried to make me part of her exciting life. She tried.

Meanwhile, I was in awe at our recent and abundant household
possessions: the magical answering machine that saved us from
unwanted familial calls, the VCR, the CD player, the computer.
Meanwhile I was having to play my music in the car, or at home
only when Joan wasn't around, or very low, so that she wouldn't
hear it if she happened to be around and I just couldn't resist the
urge for some Raphael or Manzanero. My only cherished traces of
the past, I thought, those corny and "dishonest" singers, remnants
that I felt forced to hide as if they were a terrible and shameful
drug addiction. My private, onanistic pleasure. Trashy memories
of underdevelopment.

⋆   ⋆   ⋆

See her there, in the kitchen, making a potato salad? Notice the
carrots she's slicing, the steak she's broiling? The lovely Rosita, ex-
Cuban refugee recently-made US citizen, is cooking dinner for her
lover. She was too much of a grown-up when she came to the
Promised Land, too old to become a true Gringa, too young to
embody the Guantanamera myth.

The lovely Rosita confessed to herself, one glorious and liberat-
ing day, that she was a lesbian. She broke out of her Cuban closet

and invaded the Night of American Pleasures. Finally free. Life was this endless chain of women. Later, after she fell in love, so to speak, life was this union, this sort of "marriage," this matrimonial bliss.

Do you see her in the kitchen? She's really an average girl, this Rosita from Guantánamo. She never gets depressed. She doesn't ask existential questions, has no tormenting conflicts. She's lucky.

Bathing in the steaming, bubbly water of her condo's jacuzzi, fed up with the smog and her chronic inertia, Rosita thinks of herself as a renegade hedonist. She laughs at her family, she says they are a dying race, a soon-to-be-extinct species. She's playful and brutal, proudly and gladly unpatriotic. There are no traces of the past in her luxurious Seal Beach pad (except for an occasional song by Raphael). Vaginal and tantalizing Georgia O'Keeffes on the walls, no maps of the Crocodile-Island, no flags, no black beans no *picadillo* no *yuca* and no *mercocha*. No one screams *coño* in this house. No one longs for a return to the way things used to be. In her condo's jacuzzi she laughs at her lost-generation parents, at her philosophical grandmother, at her much-too-macho Republican brother.

She splits her sides laughing, hysterically, when she thinks about the Cuban Club José Martí, ironically named after the great poet and apostle: her father playing dominoes with three other Papi look-alikes, her mother and grandmother gossiping away in some corner of the creme-de-la-creme room, and Pedro playing the Cuban stud with the beautiful and untouchable-before-marriage *Cubanitas*, his typical medallion with the Virgin of Charity hanging from his neck, displayed over his hairy chest. Pedro, who rapidly lost the Castilian accent he picked up in Spain and who now sounded more Cuban than Ricky Ricardo, if that were possible. Pedro who still talked without pauses, long strings of sentences in which the ghastly phrase *oye, chico* was patriotically interpolated every two words. Pedro, the real estate agent who still lived at home and who still ate his Mami's food.

The unavoidable Cuban Cow Club Questions:

"*OYE, CHICA*, ROSITA, WHEN ARE WE GOING TO MEET YOUR BOYFRIEND?"

"*OYE, CHICA*, ROSITA, WHEN ARE YOU GOING TO GIVE US THE PLEASURE OF ATTENDING YOUR WEDDING?"

"*OYE, CHICA*, ROSITA, AREN'T YOU WORRIED THAT YOU'RE GETTING TOO OLD FOR MARRIAGE? AREN'T YOU CONCERNED?"

"DON'T YOU LIKE ANY OF THESE HANDSOME CUBAN
BOYS? ALL THESE FINE AND DECENT ELIGIBLE YOUNG
BACHELORS?"
"*OYE, CHICA*, ROSITA, HOW COME YOU HARDLY EVER
COME TO THE CLUB?"
"AREN'T YOU BECOMING TOO MUCH OF A GRINGA,
ROSITA?"
*OYE, CHICA*, ROSITA!!

⋆  ⋆  ⋆

She's a true antiheroic image, a liberated thirtysomething human being with no ties and no roots anywhere. She teaches the
Spanish language without a Cuban accent because that pays the
mortgage; she teaches Latin American short stories by lunatic writers like Borges, Márquez and Cortázar, because they're part of her
Department's curriculum. (But at home she reads small-press Lesbian novels, the ones verging on porno.)

She gulps down two cups of watered-down coffee every morning and sits alone in a hamburger joint five days a week. Do you
see her? She's happy. Through the drive-in restaurant's glass wall,
she's happy to see the landscape of supermarkets, oil wells, park-
ing lots, aesthetically mowed lawns and entertaining garage sales.
Happy to be part of this booming, advanced universe.

Happy.

# Eight

IT WAS HIM. Older, slightly smaller; his hair thinner and his eyes cloudier. But it was him, forcing me to watch him pee into the puddle again, or pull back the skin of his red head. I had dreamed about this moment for years. Yes, I wanted to avenge the little boy I used to know. To make things better for him. To say: here's that man at your feet: Hernando. Do what you want with him.

My fantasy: I'd find him by chance in a bus, walking down the street, in a bar, at a party, through a friend of a friend, I would find him. And I'd be his child again, his Cuban Hansel, his divine Gidon. And he would again be my Protector. He would save me from the wolves, from other hungry beasts.

I pull apart my cheeks for him; he penetrates me. Once upon a time he said I'd love it. And I do. I'm loving it. I love it yes I love it. There's no pain. It doesn't hurt at all. And I can't get enough of it. Make it grow and swell inside of me, please. Make it invade me. He knows how to do it, he has expertise. How lucky I am to have found him. Little boys like me need a powerful man like Hernando. I should bless my good fortune.

I went back to him many times. I lived in terror thinking of Pipo, imagining Pipo's reaction if he ever found out. I lived in terror thinking of Hernando, imagining myself butchered by the *machete* he used to cut off the plantain bunches. My little bloody pieces spread over the floor of his hut, over his cot and over his prick.

Hernando's wrath and Pipo's wrath.

Blackmailed into committing a crime against my body. Eager and reluctant; threatened and forced, curious; feeling sinful, self-conscious and spiteful; embittered, impassioned, prematurely aware of my human form, I went back to him.

Fidel had emptied out his jails and had poured the scum into the Mariel port, crowding up boat after boat with undesirable filth. Not one but a hundred ships of fools, crews of madmen. And homosexuals. Happy to be throwing out his rotten garbage, making room for the clean and the strong and the straight and the healthy. Making room for good revolutionary morals in his obsolete paradise, Fidel sent Hernando my way. The Marielito.

He didn't recognize me. How could he? I cruised him and he fell for my game, head first into my trap. He was probably thinking how lucky he got, landing a sexy babe like me who looked more Gringo than Cuban, how lucky. He could see himself licking the shit off my blonde ass already, plunging his tongue into my tight hole already. He could almost taste me.

He told me he was out of work, that he could use a hand. He had been living with this American sponsor but the guy had kicked him out. He was a skinny white *pájaro* who screamed all the time, for no reason, and who fondled his poodle compulsively. A good-for-nothing Gringo who said that he, Hernando, was a lazy bum. But Hernando was only going to do decent work. He wasn't about to be cleaning out people's bathrooms and handling dog shit. Not him. Not Hernando. He was happy he'd met me and that I had a job for him.

Yes, a dignified job, Hernando. And I am very happy to have met you, too, here in Little Havana, Union City. Lucky for you. Lucky for me. Yes, I'll pay your train fare to New York, I'll get you clothes and food and you can stay with me for as long as you need to. I live with someone. He's cool, *buena gente*. He won't mind your staying over. I'll get you back on your feet, Hernando. This is a land of freedom and progress. Be glad you came to us. *Mi casa es tu casa.*

Make yourself at home.

He stares at my face looking for Marito but he doesn't see him. He trusts me, I can tell. But should he? Should he let me show him to the bedroom? Should he let me serve him a Cuba Libre, offer him a comfortable robe, slippers?

Shouldn't he be more cautious? Shouldn't he suspect that I have a plan, that I spiked his beverage, that in a matter of minutes he'll be dozing off and falling on the floor, that in a matter of minutes I will drag his body to the bed and tie it up?

He should know better than to let himself be picked up by a stranger in The City.

Reality wins. Reality is better. There he is, sprawled on my bed, naked. For real. His wrists and his ankles chained, his mouth gagged, his eyes awakening to the horror of his situation.

And now he sees me. He sees the boy I used to be. And he

cries, and he tries to break away. His body convulses, shrivels up. I shall make it burn. I shall awaken its ancestral and most horrifying memories. I shall inhabit its pores. I shall bite it and scratch it and poke it and abuse it. I shall inscribe my name on it with my teeth: *Marito.*

I have been waiting for your nervous tic and your coughing, Hernando. For your straight black hair and thin eyebrows, your aquiline nose, your lipless mouth. For your hairy arms and your soft, rubbery stomach, Hernando. I have looked for your big balls and huge dick everywhere, longing for the masculine juice of a man like you, a man who fucks women. I have been waiting ...

You knew I was a faggot from the moment you laid eyes on me. Kids like me need special attention, isn't that it? We're fragile and delicate, weaker than girls. Only a man like you can help us, right? Give us the special protection we require. Thank you for not telling on me. Thank you for not telling anybody that I gave you my ass.

Yes you saw my future. I have been a baby all my life. I'm bigger now, but I'm still a baby. I have developed muscles and my thighs have gotten bigger. You should touch them, they're still firm and tender, the flesh of a boy who eats well. Here, feel them. I am your passive and obedient child.

And if you let me stick my knife under your skin, just a little bit, like this, if you let me, I swear I'll do anything for you, Hernando. What a good man you are, letting me cut your soft skin. Now you must let me drive my knife through here, yes, back here, your little round cheeks, so soft and warm. And now if you give me your hand, put it here, see? You can move it inside, the fly is open, try it. Put your hand inside, that's good. It's sharp. Have you ever touched anything as sharp as that blade? Let's bring it out, you want to? You like it don't you? Look how red the edge is getting under the lamplight. I pull back your skin like this, all the way back, look how it moves, and then your insides swell up. I lick them, I eat them. I'll do anything for you, Hernando. I swear. Anything.

◇   ◇   ◇

Purple lips, my hair combed back and burnished. I couldn't speak: my most enticing trait was silence. If I uttered the slightest sound my gleaming teeth would protrude. And I couldn't show them to just anybody. Not just yet.

I danced with all the other creatures, always keeping a distance, painfully aware of my alleged intangibility. I drank a bittersweet concoction made of cherries and tequila. I drank it in slow, premeditated gulps, letting it quench my thirst, alleviate the heat that my disguise was producing. I tried, in vain, to seem undaunted. I sought and found the darkest niche in that old Victorian house, upstairs, and there I sat, drinking, sulking and nourishing my fantasy.

The music reached my ears. A mellow, faintly audible voice humming what sounded like a child's song. Then the lyrics, hard to make out, that brought into my solitude images of tenebrous blind alleys. The beat of the song was hard-driving, pounding electric drums and synthesizer strings. No harmony between orchestration and voice. And yet it all worked into a whole, a haunting whole. She was a little girl in the woods, carefree and happy, whispering her words into my ear. But her soundtrack was played by a powerful and morbid phantom. How could such assonance be so perfect?

I heard laughter. My fellow freaks downstairs, inebriated and abandoned, rejoicing in their moment of flight. No place for thinking. Or for feeling. Obliteration time. Were they ready for me? Would I show my true colors at this hour? I was afraid. There had been no indication of his presence yet. I hadn't *seen* him.

*You must appear in human form*, I heard myself say. As I started my descent into the party, I glanced at my face in the mirror. It was blatantly visible. A dilapidated creature, corroded by years of aimless sex and insomnia, crushed by the knowledge of his mortality. Not a nocturnal spirit. Just me alone with all my fears and all my fantasies. Another one of the thousand and one masks haunting the old San Francisco mansion this night of Halloween. There was no trick or treat for me. Only self-pity. What a pathetic reflection, that paleness glaring back at me, laughing and poking fun at me. Where was *his* face?

I ran out, my cloak writhing behind me and hoisting itself like a mercenary flag. Desperate for air and desperate for life, I ran. Had I become a true vampire? Was that the reason that the night was such a soothing balm? I belonged in it. My truest realization: I had never been able to cope with the light. The sun was my torturer, my executioner. And I had never felt as free as I did now, out in the open, thrust into the dark like a targetless bullet.

The trees were new to me. The moon was a novel vision, too. A spark of life burned in my heart, I touched it. I reached inside and held on to it, letting myself be burned and blinded by its candescent aura. I stopped and looked around, pleased by the theatricality of my exit.

Memories of the party flooded my mind. I had never stopped acting my part, while I was there, impersonating the frightful blood-sucker like a true diva. No one had noticed my apprehension, the cold sweat trickling down my spine. Behind the image of the handsome and alluring *Homme Fatale* I was trembling. Behind the suave veneer there was a homeless boy, a little man incapable of killing, driven solely by his need to see His Holy Spirit become flesh.

Was this the end of my farce? Where would I go now? After giving the greatest performance of his life, the comedian rips the glamorous mask off his face and turns into a bird. Up and away he flies, reaching the highest branches, making his nest. Or is it a web? Whatever it was I had become, a bird, a human bat, a fool, a naive neomystic, I was here. Ready for the finale.

But what if the object of my quest didn't exist? Would I go back to my casket, resigned to dream away the hours of my nightly death, alone? I couldn't accept the fact that this was just another masquerade, that I would never have proof of his benevolence. An unbearable thought. Unacceptable. I was not prepared for failure. He would be there and I would guide him. He would feel the pleasurable thrust of my bite, follow me to the silence of my grave. I knew he would.

Yes, he had been here all along, just like me, inhabiting the dusty cracks of the wooden walls, swirling through the sweaty bodies like a mischievous wind-child. He had watched me attentively while I played my vampy role. He was afraid, like me, to break the spell, to let the inevitable truth of our encounter take its course. So he observed me in silence. Blending in with the boisterous crowd, he described every one of my gestures, my sadness-riddled glances to himself. He sensed my flight but didn't follow me into the night.

He waited. He knew I would come back for him.

And I did. Just when the body of disguises was beginning to thin out. When only those creatures willing to wait for dawn together, all-in-one, remained. A joke about what I was probably doing in the bushes: Stalking a hunky and horny victim? Sinking my teeth into his juicy neck? Jokes about me, the master of lusty transformations, had a way of proliferating endlessly.

I collapsed on the couch and pretended to stop breathing. Peaceful, tranquil sleep came to me almost immediately. The sounds of sex were not a nuisance. I was used to sleeping in the midst of passionate encounters. Thriving tongues, inundated crevices, sloppy caresses were for me like ocean waves rocking me back and forth, enhancing my own oniric pleasure.

Wake up. Let's go home, he said.

But I am home. This is my house. These people are my friends. They love me and admire my flair, my talent for turning the worst situation into victory. They come to me when they need rescuing. I go to them when I need to be saved. Believe me, they will never betray me. This is home.

But he knew the truth. He embraced me and I wept in his arms. I felt amorphous and unusually warm next to his thin physique, wrapped in his long and hairless legs, touching his lips, soft and ample, the tiny eyelids, the character lines that enclosed his mouth, his red hair; I was unusually warm next to him, agitating in circles with my index finger the minuscule ringlets that grew from his temples.

I didn't really want his sex. The tone of his voice yes, perhaps, unsure and defensive, but willing; the tender way in which he held me. Tenderness, I thought. Oh how I crave it. I bite his nipples tenderly, I hold his hand, kiss his long white fingers tenderly. He rests his head on my chest, curious and bewildered, words pouring out of him in endless succession; whispered words, words drowning in our kisses tenderly. I savor his tongue, I inhale him, unable to believe that I can finally possess his human form.

⋄    ⋄    ⋄

I called up and made the appointment from your house. And the woman said Good luck. When I asked her for the phone number of the clinic she said Call them up right away, it won't cost you anything, it's a free program set up by the state for anyone who considers himself or herself in the high-risk group. If you feel ready then do it, she said. Have the test. Good luck, my friend.

They showed me tapes. Video tapes of people who didn't want to have the test and people who did. Testimonials and that sort of thing. They wanted to make sure that I knew what I was up against.

You watched the tapes with me and when the doctor or the nurse or whoever it was called my number, you shivered, you hugged me. Could they have thought you were my sister?

The weather was pleasant. There was smog, I remember. It was a smoggy summer day. Hot, maybe. And we were wearing shorts. Your hair was fluffy and smooth; I touched it, played with it. That habit of yours, you said. Yes, that habit of mine. The people I love, I play with their hair, teasing it and making tiny braids out of it. And you let me, Rosi, while we were watching those people talk about their fears and the hell they went through waiting for the test results, you let me play with your hair.

One week, they said. That's how long it takes. Then you know. You come back and we give you the results. But make sure you spend that week with someone you love. A relative who cares. Or your spouse.

So you called in sick at your college. Your students wouldn't miss you. Lucky for me you were willing to pamper me for seven days.

We played all your oldies, Los Memes, Los Bravos, Manzanero, Massiel, Raphael. The music that I had forgotten or that I never knew. We danced and sang all week. And we watched movies, the Mexican classics that you were crazy about. And you even managed to come up with a Cuban film, *Se permuta*, starring your childhood idol, Rosita Fornés. A mature and graciously aging Rosita, no longer the glamorous *artista* but still edible, in your opinion. *Se permuta* was a fine, light-hearted comedy, just what we needed, and it amazed us both that the Cuban film industry was capable of producing such good stuff.

You cooked black beans and pork and fried plantain and you made my favorite Cuban dessert, *mercocha*. And you said that it was your favorite, too, that your Mami still made it for you. You called her up and she gave you the recipe. And it tasted so good, Rosi, better than the one my mother used to make.

The seventh day was a Friday. We were in the car and ready to drive off, and you asked me if I had the paper with my number, but I didn't. And I couldn't remember where I'd put it.

They don't know your name. They tell you from the very first moment, when the receptionist greets you. We don't want to know who you are or where you work or who your friends are. Just write down your phone number for us, that will be your identity. For the next seven days, this is who you are. But I couldn't remember my own number. So I gave them yours. I didn't think you'd mind. And minutes later a lab technician was drawing my blood. And it looked thick, bright carmine, lush, alive.

So here we were in the car and I couldn't remember where I'd put the damned piece of paper with my identification. Would they tell me anyway? Would they give me the results without my paper? They would, they'd have to. Off we went, silently. We had never been so quiet. We had always had so much to say to each other.

You did say something, seconds before you parked the car you said that if this didn't turn out the way we wanted it to, if they didn't give me good news in there, we'd find other ways. You had heard of these women, these women who could help me in ways that modern medicine couldn't. We'd go see them, we'd engage their magical powers.

Not to worry. You'd stay by my side no matter what, you told me. And I believed you. And then you stroked my arm and my hand. The health I have, you said, the love the life, the breath I have I give to you, my friend. From my skin to your skin, through your pores, my health.

You waited. They wouldn't let you in. You picked up a magazine and skimmed it, then you stared at one particular page. Was it the picture of a beautiful woman? Must've been. You didn't lift your eyes from that page until I came out. And when I did, when you heard the sound of my sandals dragging through the hallway, you froze. And I found you, split seconds before you lifted your eyes, I found you there, stricken by a terrible premonition, staring at that same page.

The doctor had called out my number, your phone number, and had courteously asked me to come into his office. He was heavy-set; his eyes were amber-grey, he was balding. He didn't give me a chance to pretend, by looking at his weary eyes, that he was about to announce wonderful news. Sit down, he said. And I sank into the cushioned chair. I would like to talk a little bit with you. Tell me, please, about your life.

I looked out the window the way I'm looking out now. The leaves seemed so green and the smoggy sky so unusually clear. His voice came as an echo, minutes, days, years later. He reached out and touched me, cutting me loose from an invisible cord that was propelling me through the clouds. Talk to me, please. Don't tell me your name, just who you are.

And for the life of me, I couldn't respond. I had no words, no thoughts, no feelings. I was a vacuous form where nothingness lived. How could I tell him who I was. Did I know? Do you know, Rosi, who I am?

The first step of the process is to be honest with myself and with him. Otherwise, how can he help me? He has a handful of advice for me. He's been through this before with other patients and he knows what to do, what to say and how to respond. These walls have no ears. I can trust him. He's not judging me, he says. He's on my side and he will see to it that I get the proper help, if I need it.

So I spill my guts out. A benevolent and sexless voyeur, he watches me as I give myself away to maleness; as I swallow and eat and choke and rim and fuck and get fucked and fucked and fucked again. And when the orgy ends, when nothing is left of all the bodies but a mound of ashes on his carpet, he rises, he walks, he moves out of his way the plant that sits on the windowsill. He sits there by the window, avoiding my eyes. And then he speaks, his hands on his lap. And I listen.

# Nine

FRIDAY EVENING. Rosita's parents and her brother Pedro are having dinner in their modest but nicely maintained Garden Shore residence. They are devouring meatballs, pork chops, *picadillo*, ham croquettes, black bean soup, white rice, fried plantain slices, bread pudding, *flan*, *natilla*, *mercocha*. They are drinking beer, Pop Cola, wine, banana daiquiris, Cuba Libres, buckets of sweet thick Cuban coffee.

They are talking about Castro. About the deteriorated state of the Cuban economy, the undeniable fact that the bearded pig's days are numbered, the blatant fact that Communism is a dead beast; about how good life used to be in Guantánamo and how expensive it is getting to be in California; about the smog, the traffic; about how nice the garden has been looking lately and how difficult it has been to keep the swimming pool clean; about how proud they are of Pedrito for doing so well in his prestigious real estate profession, for having found such a lovely and domesticated and patriotic Cuban girl, his pretty girlfriend; about how happy they would be if he settled down and gave them five Pedritos; about how happy they would be if Rosita found a good man and settled down and gave them ten grandsons; about how happy they would be—or would they?—if they could all go back to Guantánamo some day.

At the sacred hour of coffee Rosita shows up. She looks distressed and pale; she's dragging her feet. Her family welcomes her the usual *Oye chica* way, with kisses and hugs and it's been such a long time since you've come to see your folks and sit down with us and have something to eat there's lots left please have at least a bite. She declines, accepting only a cup of espresso. She needed to see them, she says. She needed to be with her family today.

"Is something wrong, dear?" her Mami inquires, handing her a steaming cup of *cafecito*. "Are you sick?" "No, no, I'm not sick." And Rosita wonders what she's doing here. Her parents would never understand. But who in the world would? Joan? She hasn't been around lately, totally consumed by a multi-million dollar soft drink commercial for SAP. Who, then? Her brother? Flashes of life in Spain, centuries ago, with Pedro. Does he ever think about it? He was a chubby little boy who lisped like an authentic Spaniard. He thought Tía Lola was a mummy, *una momia*! And he hated the heavy old coat he was forced to wear; it made him look poor, he said, like a lottery vendor. He went to confession on Sundays and told the priest his "bad" sins of the week, *los malos pecados*. As if there were "good" ones. Devout and confirmed Catholic children, Pedrito and Rosita, because that's what they were expected to be. What did they know about religion? About God? Could she turn to God now? Unearth Him, blow the dust off her pious memories and pray again? Would that help?

"Something is wrong with you, Rosi. I just know it," she hears her Mami say, lovingly and genuinely concerned. "Are you working too much?" "Nah!" Pedro interjects, "teaching isn't hard work!" "That's right," says Rosita, trying to contain her tears, "I don't bust my ass like you, selling all those mansions and condos ... from the cellular phone in your BMW ... Such slavery!" "I was only joking, Rosi!" her brother states, unusually apologetic. "I know you work hard, *coño!*" And his sympathetic remark is the final straw, she can't hold back any longer. "*Ay* Mami!" she cries out, hiding her face in her hands. "I'm sorry, Rosita!" Pedro runs to her side. "Since when are you so sensitive, *chica*?!" He offers her his handkerchief, which he always carries in the right back pocket of his pants, like a good Cuban man.

"What is it, Rosi?!" her Mami asks, crying. "Tell me what's wrong!" And Rosita Rodríguez, *la guantanamera*, tells her family the reason why she's so distraught. One phrase. One simple phrase: "My best friend is dying."

★ ◇ ★

"Did you call him?"
"Yes. I begged him to come see me."
"What did he say?"
"The same thing he always says ... that I am not his son."
"And your mother?"
"Locked up ... She doesn't even recognize me."
"A case of poetic injustice."
"Let me just go to sleep, Rosi ... It feels so good to be in bed ... "
"Is he there with you?"
"Yes ... and I'm touching his chest, hairy and warm ... "
"And what is he doing?"

"Looking at me ... smiling ... I think he loves me."

"And does he?"

"No."

"How do you know?"

"Because ... "

"How do you know he doesn't love you?"

"I feel ... his blows."

"Why does he hit you?"

"Because ... "

"Why?"

"Because I told all the kids in the barrio about our brand new TV set .... Because I hide in the back room and lock the door ... Because I ran away from home with a neighbor kid and I was gone for hours, sitting under a tamarind tree with him, kissing the palms of his hands ... Because I sprawl all over the chair as if I had a pussy to air out ... Because I like to draw pictures of naked toy-brothers ... Because I look and act like a girl."

"Tell him to stop hitting you."

"I can't."

"Tell him, Marito."

"I can't! My voice doesn't come out ... "

"Speak to him with your eyes, then."

"I can't."

"But you love him, don't you?"

"Let me forget him!"

"Not yet. Tell him you love him first."

"He was just sick. A normal father could never treat a son that way ... a loving father would never do ... what he did to me ... Tell me I'm right, Rosi ... "

"You are."

"I wish ... I could cry."

"Try it."

"I can't."

"Just relax ... "

"If I ... If I love him ... why does he hate me?"

"Maybe he doesn't hate you."

"No ... "

"Maybe he thinks he's doing the right thing."

"I don't want to have to need him ... I don't like feeling so helpless."

"Nobody likes feeling helpless, Marito."

"Someone told me once that I'd always be a child ... Some son of a bitch told me that ... But he was wrong, wasn't he?"

"He was."

"I hate being a child."

★  ◇  ★

Truth is, that Friday afternoon I drove aimlessly through Los Angeles. I played my tapes during rush hour; I sang the song about "Sweethearts" at the top of my lungs, trying to resist the urge to run home and tell my folks. Oh how I longed to hide in my Mami's bosom, to hold her tight and tell her Mami I love you, please save me protect me tell me life is good tell me it is worth living. I could've done that and maybe, just maybe she would've understood.

But I didn't. Instead, I let my car take me to the hamburger joint where I eat twice a week. I ordered a diet Pop Cola and sat in a corner. I must've been crying copiously, judging from the looks I was getting. A man sitting across from me came over and asked me if there was something wrong. A good Samaritan. I almost told him, No dude, what could possibly be wrong? This is the way I normally react to this food. I thanked him for his concern and amiably asked him to leave me alone.

That morning we had been given the results of your test. I had dropped you off at my place, leaving you behind to cope with your truth alone. I told you I needed to run a few errands. Good, you nodded, you needed some time by yourself. I joined you hours later, when the sun had already set and I thought I was prepared. You welcomed me with a hug. What a day, huh? you said. What a fucking day, I added. We were both prepared.

You suggested we go to the beach and take a walk, or write a poem on the sand, like the one we wrote the night we met. *Before I found you, I inhabited hell ...* No. We'll have to write a better one, you said. Better because it'll be the last one. And I begged you not to think that way. We're gonna fight this off, Marito! We're gonna fight it off and win! But you were beyond false hope and optimism, way out there on the other side of life.

★  ◇  ★

"I like it when it gets dark like this, Rosi ... And I can see your face in chiaroscuro. Your body ... so perfect in a swimming suit, baring your belly button ... long legs, dark and firm, tanned to bronze ... your eyes jet black, your short straight hair ... My Cuban girl."

"Your Cuban woman."

"Put on your swimming suit for me. Will you?"

"Done. Should we go to the jacuzzi?"

"No ... I want to draw a little ... "

"Here's pencil and paper."

"Smooth surface ... On the white surface a cat ... jaundiced eyes ... a subway station ... a subterranean train ... the rails ... "

"Where is the train taking you?"

"I'm going home. He waits for me in his apartment ... listening to Willie and Lucecita ... He's a ghetto grade school teacher ... but he wants to be a writer ... Will his dream come true?"

"I don't know, Marito."

"I make him a chocolate milk shake and he gets excited about it, like a kid ... He's a chocoholic, did you know? On Sunday afternoons we stroll through Central Park ... Or we go visit his revolutionary friends ... Or he reads me his poetry. I love his poems, even if I don't understand them."

"Does he love your paintings?"

"Yes, yes. And I'm painting a lot. His love has inspired me ... I work in a loft with wooden floors and wall-size windows, a spacious and uncluttered studio ... He tells me that I'll make it in the Big Apple ... But I know I won't ... And I know he'll leave me one day."

"No. You'll leave him."

"Not true! I loved him."

"Maybe that's why you left."

"Is he alive, Rosi?"

"Here, in your heart."

"He died?"

"Yes."

"So many people dying ... Is Jimmy dead, too?"

"No. Not Jimmy."

"Jimmy's a survivor. He will survive the Plague."

"Is he with you now?"

"Having breakfast with me, yes ... I tell him I'm an artist and he seems impressed ... "

"But you're not really an artist. Or are you?"

"I reflect reflections ... Is that art?"

"I wouldn't know."

"God, I want to make love to Jimmy!"

"Would that take your pain away?"

"It would, for a while ... "

"Then find him this instant and make love to him."

"Little boy lost in my arms ... "

"Where are you?"

"At the beach, watching him swim ... He's calling me, asking me to jump in."

"Do you love him?"

"Yes ... I love him."

"How do you feel now?"

"Better ... But I wish I could cry for Jimmy."

"Jimmy doesn't need your tears. He's a survivor, remember?"

"He won't fall!"

"And if he falls, you'll save him."

"And who will save me, Rosi?"

"I will."

★  ◇  ★

We sat near the water, that Friday, and you rested your head on my thighs. Imagine the orgy I'm gonna start up in Heaven, you told me, laughing. *Oye, chico*, I said, forcing my laughter, and without me!

But sooner or later we'll meet up again, right? I want you to give me a spectacular reception, Marito, with a choir of cherubs and cupids singing my name. Yes, Rosi, very feminine cherubs and cupids, with hard little nipples. But what about the ones who will receive me, Rosi? What will they look like?

You ran your hands down your face. My skin, you cried, it's so dry, feel it. Trying to laugh again, feeling your dryness, I told you that you had sexier cheek bones, now that you were finally turning into La Fornés. A miracle! But you were feeling tired, too tired for jokes. If only you could just stay here with me forever, listening to the ocean. My hands are nice, yes, they feel cool on your face.

But what about the poem, Marito? We can't write it now, it's gotten dark. Can we sleep here, Rosi? Sure, why not. We'll write our poem in the morning, when the day breaks.

You said you once knew a man who had died without a god to comfort him. He expected nothing of the other world. *There is no other world*, the man used to say. He would turn into dust and vanish. His deeds would remain. But what good would they be to him once he was gone? Not a fucking bit of good.

Now you found yourself turning to God, painting him on your walls. A virile messiah. In the flesh, not the spirit, with no crown of thorns and no cross and no pain. Now you prayed, hoping to seize his human form again. And you searched for a word, a name to give him in your secret thoughts. A name to pleasure you. What should I call him? you asked. *Padre*?

★ ◇ ★

"I'm drawing again, Rosi!"

"Yes. A tamarind tree and a flower."

"Thick, sweet raindrops, coconut water ... dark clouds, a body of leaves, fine fingers, the legs of a spider ... puddles and mud, tadpoles ... garments of cilantro ... my freedom ... "

"Where are you, Marito?"

"In a parish church ... I think ... "

"What are you doing?"

"Nothing ... One of the altar boys is looking at me ... "

"Do you like him?"

"He knows the ritual by heart ... He's been confirmed, you know ... He doesn't beat around the bush. He asks, 'Do you want to suck my dick?' But I don't."

"Then don't. Go on. Where are you?"

"At home ... hiding in the bathroom ... looking at my face in the mirror."

"What do you see?"

"A monster."

"Are you bleeding?"

"Yes ... And I'm touching my cuts."

"Do you hear anything?"

"Yes. His voice."

"What is he saying?"

"He's talking with Mima."

"What are they talking about?"

"He's telling her that we'll have to leave soon ... That this is turning into a fucking living hell ... And she's saying that Fidel had everybody fooled, that he's not an angel and a savior but a mean devil ... "

"Why are you laughing?"

"Because it's funny."

"What? What's funny?"

"The way they talk and act ... They're so scared!"

"And you're not?"

"I don't fear Fidel ... the way they do."

"You don't?"

"No ... I have already known ... a greater dictator."

"Are you still in the bathroom?"

"Yes."

"Get out of there. Let's leave Guantánamo. Where should we go?"

"I don't know ... I'm here already."

"Where?"

"In Hollywood ... The Hustling Zone ... A small rats' nest on Selma Street ... "

"What are you doing?"

"Smoking and walking in front of what used to be Caesar's. My first tricks ... the naked dancers ... porno flicks on the walls ... all-around and sensurround fucking ... a song that kills me softly ... "

"Don't stay there."

"It's easy in Hollywood ... Always easy."

"Get out."

"They're waiting in line for me, Rosi."

"Who? Who's waiting in line?"

"The boys at the barracks ... They're all waiting their turn ... in front of my cot."

"What are they waiting their turn for?"

"You know ... "

"And do you want them to do it?"

"I'd love it."

"What if your father finds out?"

"My father? I don't have a father."

"You do, Marito. And he will kill you if ... "

"I don't care! I'll defend myself! I'll fight back!"

"Okay. Let the boys fuck you, then."

"They promise they'll never tell on me. Tattletales are punished by stoning ... This will be our secret ... "

"I love secrets."

"And I love sitting here on the floor ... with you."

"Where are you?"

"On the porch of a chalet. There's a rose garden and a lemon tree and there's a little girl by the window, singing. She's dressed in pink lace and white bows ... pretty ... I'm listening, looking at her, applauding ... applaud ... applauding ... app ... app ... "

"What's the matter?!"

"Let me go!"

"Why? Why are you running?!"

"Steps behind me ... "

"Don't run, Mario. You don't have to run."

"But I do! I've gotta get to my house!"

"You're there already. At home. Safe."

"Gun shots ... and sirens. My mother warned me, Don't go near the War Zone! Play all you want, but stay away from the Guantánamo fence ... Don't cross the fence!"

"But you crossed it."

"I did ... That's why I'm lost ... And dead."

"You may be lost. But dead you're not. Feel my fingers going through your hair. My lips on your rosy nails, on your dove-hands, Marito. Feel them."

★   ◇   ★

CLUB CUBANO JOSE MARTI. Should you go in? Yes, make a theatrical entrance. You're wearing a rose-colored costume, tight and low-cut, Monroe-style; your face hidden behind a thin green veil; your blonde hair pulled back in a chignon; high cheek bones, defying eyes caressed by the penumbra.

The women are talking about you. They're shooting their words at you like machine-gun fire, coffee dripping from their thick carmine lips. Human hippos crushing your monkeys, your zebras, your giraffes, your horses, dogs, cows, bulls, sheep, kangaroos, your doves and their nests and eggs and everything.

One of them says you should see a doctor. Or a priest. But a doctor for sure, because you need help. *Silk screens, the same profile* ... because you look and act too much like a woman. *On the grass, naked* ... But that's what you are! And a man says that you don't need no doctor, that he's gonna make you normal with his fists. They talk about you as if you weren't there. *On the grass.* As if you were invisible. *Naked* ...

THE CLUB AGAINST MARIO! ACCUSED OF PATRICIDE.

IN THE NAME OF THE SACRED CUBAN LAW WE ORDER YOU TO SPEAK!

DID YOU OR DID YOU NOT KILL YOUR FATHER?!

WHY DID YOU KILL HIM?

WHY?!

The jury members, all men, admire your astonishing beauty. They will never throw a lady in jail. You're not ashamed of your crime. Go ahead, lie down on the chaise-lounge; smoke through your long filter, slow, sensuous drags of perfumed smoke. Yes, lie down and dream. Tonight as one thousand and one nights ago: A reflection that shatters. You must rip him off your skin. Do it before the twelfth stroke, before it's too late to return to who you are. To who you want to be.

★   ◇   ★

"Don't you just love my dress, Rosi? It's pink and tight and I'm wearing a fur coat ... I look radiant!"

"Yes. Like a delicate rose. Where are you?"

"In a little village. It's carnival time ... I'm taking a promenade on my lover's arm. His name is Amor. He's very Catholic and very handsome ... And I am his decent girl ... "

"But doesn't he know?"

"What? What is he supposed to know?"

"That you're not really his innocent girl."

"You're right. I am the Carnival Queen, and he doesn't know it ... So I guess ... I guess our love is doomed."

"Unless ... "

"Yes?"

"Unless you tell him the truth and he accepts you the way you are."

"That would be sweet ... He wouldn't have to die because of my horrible truth ... He wouldn't be swallowed up by the sea ... *Amor*! Say you forgive me!"

"But there's nothing to forgive."

"Say you accept me, then."

"I do."

"Say that you love me."

"I do. Now will you sing your song?"

"From the moment the day is born, to the moment when the sun dies, *Amor*, my love, I think of you ... *Amor*, my love, you live in my heart ... "

"Here. Have some *mercocha*."

"Did you make it, Rosi?"

"Yes. I made it for you."

"Rosi ... "

"Yes?"

"Can I kiss you?"

"Okay. But only a little kiss. You know I don't like to kiss boys."

"Fantastic, because I don't like to kiss girls ... but I would love to kiss you ... because you're my sister."

"I am, Marito. I am."

"Get me out of here, please!"

"Out of where?"

"Out of this convent ... "

"You're in a convent?"

"Yes ... Ragged men are staining the white-washed walls with their filthy paws ... crushing the flowers ... shattering our holy silence ... "

"Who are these men?!"

"I don't know ... Bandits ... They tear off our habits, drowning us in their stench, making us suffer their assault ... our first time, in horror ... "

"Don't let them!"

"Nine months later ... Nine ... months later ... "

"Go on, Mario."

"Coming out of a coma ... "

"Go on."

"I struggle to get up and I peek out the window ... catching a glimpse of the courtyard down below ... and witnessing the burial of a tiny casket ... Chanting. I hear the nuns chanting ... The Liturgy of Death ... White habits glisten ... Is that my son in the casket? The stillborn son of a bandit?"

"No, I don't think so."

"Let me go!"

"Not yet. Stay here. Stay and tell me what you see."

"Flowers ... lots of flowers ... And four strangers lifting up the casket ... "

"A tiny casket?"

"No ... It's hot, really hot. We're sweating. But we walk. It's a procession ... And we get there, to the wrought iron gate ... they're still excavating. The box into the hole, ropes ... The box is heavy."

"Where are you?"

"Standing in front of the hole."

"What are you doing?"

"My hand is reaching out to him ... Down to him."

"Can you touch him?"

"No ... My chest ... my chest is making a strange noise."

"You're crying."

"They cover the hole little by little, they fill it up with dirt ... No trace of the box. No trace ... "

"Why are you crying, Marito?"

"Because ... "

"Why?"

"I can't breathe!"

"Yes, you can!"

"I'm afraid."

"There's nothing to fear."

"People go by, they don't care that I'm crying, they can't help me find Pipo ... I need to be carried by him, I want to listen to his singing ... tie his shoes, hear his laughter because I make too many knots, because I don't do it right, the way you're supposed to ... I just need to see my Pipo!"

"You must forgive him first."

"He turned his back on me!"

"Forgive him."

"Why? I'm not God."

"No. But you're my greatest friend."

"Clinging to you, clinging to you I cling to him ... as if afraid that you might leave me ... that you might hide from me ... "

"And he tells you that it was all a prank, that he will never hide from you again because he loves you and he doesn't want to hurt you."

"Pipo's hand on my face, wiping off my tiny tears with his fingers ... Lost little boy is pouting ... My tears on his lips, he

# Ten

WE ARE IN CALIFORNIA. At The Laguna, to be more precise. Nice to meet you. You're from Guantánamo?! Me too! How long ago? Yes, yes, I don't look or sound Cuban at all. I would've never guessed.

We finally meet today, 1978, we actually meet for the first time at The Laguna.

I called you or you called me the next day. And we went to the beach, and we compared stories, didn't we? I showed you my old snapshots, had you listen to my Spanish albums. You showed me your landscapes and your portraits.

Our reunion couldn't have been complete without a poem that we composed together, written on the sand, and without a promise to always be friends ... *Before I found you my hands were ice. They melted away under a foreign sun. I would await, awake, the moon's caress. The soothing night. I feared the light before I met you. I inhabited hell* ...

We made a pact that night, didn't we? A pact with the God of Diversion: Here, young lady, here is the masculine physique of your soon-to-be best friend, Mario, you can have it.

Let's see, young man, let's see what you will do with this gift: the feminine and total-woman bod of your adored Rosita. For you. Have a party, live it up! Be ROSAMARIO, ROSARIO, ROSAMAR, MARITOROSA, MARIROSA, MARIPOSA! But do not forget to repossess your original form before the stroke of midnight.

There, in your Laguna shack where a Sugar Daddy or public charity kept you, we escaped from reality. You: from a faceless, extraordinarily endowed lover who would eventually contaminate you (we've got to blame somebody). I: from a lover who never took the time to smell the Real Rose, and who would eventually threaten to sue me for slander: "How dare you write about our sex life!"

After searching Heaven and Earth for a true love, for a generous homeland, for a family who wouldn't abuse us or condemn us, for a body who wouldn't betray our truest secrets, we found each other: a refuge, a song, a story to share.

⋆   ⋆   ⋆

We're not in a bar, swallowing smoke and listening to hysterical moans by The Disco Queen. No sweaty bodies are rubbing against us. You never lived in Miami or New York or California. Your mother didn't have to be locked up in a mental asylum. Your father didn't remarry, turning his back on you.

Joan didn't move out when you moved in. I didn't quit my job and I didn't live off my savings for nearly a year, taking care of you. I didn't have to be your loving nurse and you didn't have to feel grateful.

You found fame and fortune, *you made it*. Ivy League, a brilliant career. You became a lawyer or a doctor or an engineer or an accountant or a real estate agent, maybe even a Spanish professor. You have never gone hungry. When things got rough you didn't put your body up for sale. You never hustled.

And I, I never found myself alone and violated in a cold, dark Spain. How wonderful: Never having to respond to any questions about the Red Monster. Such relief. Not longing for that island that we lost, that we thought we were burying forever one day in the late nineteen-sixties.

We were made in test tubes and we were able to choose, as adults, the identity and gender that we fancied. Then we were free, until the moment of our deaths (painless deaths) to change from man to woman, from woman to man, from tree to flower, from ocean water to ivy. Better yet: we have existed from time immemorial as air.

It's a sunny day and there's an intense greenness all around us. Clean smell. You can breathe in the blue sky, the white clouds. A slow-moving brook goes through the woods, not far from where we stand. You can see the tops of palm trees, mops of silky hair fading into the horizon.

We never heard of Castro. (Not even Castro Street). Nobody hides, waving a dagger in the air, behind the mask of God.

A plague hasn't broken out.

You and I have become air. We can sneak, if we so desire, through the cracks of a rock, through minuscule grains of sand, through the wings of a bird.

There, on that solitary prairie overflowing with light, that's where we met. I was resting on the grass. You came close and said that you had lost your way. I offered you a warm place by my side, you held my hand. Then we whispered a song to each other, "We are sweethearts ... We are ... "

Yes, I said, you are my sweetheart and I love you. And I will always see your life the way you wanted to see it, as an impassioned and original painting. I will let it come out of itself and breathe, be unique. And I will let myself dream as I invent your dream.

Yes, I will create this place where you can be who you've always wanted to be, Marito. Where You and I have become the same person. This moment of greatness, I will create it. When the performance ends. And life begins.